WIFED UP BY A WEST COAST MILLIONAIRE

PORSCHEA JADE

Wifed Up By A West Coast Billionaire

Mailing List

To stay up to date on new releases, plus get information on contests, sneak peeks, and more,

Go To The Website Below...

www.colehartsignature.com

CHAPTER ONE

Bringing the wine glass to her lips for the umpteenth time, the cold liquid touched the now smeared mess. No longer displaying pouty red lips from the lipstick she wore but something else entirely. Drinking the rest of its contents, Suki placed the glass down before reaching for the wine bottle to fill it once again, only to discover it was empty. Releasing a heavy sigh, she stood in her cute fur heels that matched the sexy lace teddy with the matching lace and fur robe that draped her body. Suki's legs ached at the sudden change in position. She had been sitting in the same spot for hours waiting on Jinx to walk through the door. She had planned the night perfectly.

Suki had come home early after a long day of appointments, getting waxed, poked, and prodded to perfection, to slave in the kitchen to cook all his favorite foods before getting dolled up and setting up the romantic candlelight dinner that sat on the table in front of her. That was at nine. Now here it was a quarter past midnight and still no sign of him. The candles had burned down completely, leaving a puddle of wax in their wake she was sure made damage she couldn't see on her wooden kitchen table through the table-cloth. The vintage bottle of wine she had placed on ice was now empty, courtesy of her, and the ice no longer holding a solid form but a puddle of cold liquid she was positive she needed to consume if she didn't want a hangover in the morning.

Five years.

Five years Suki had been married to Jinx and she wondered every day when enough was enough. Jinx had shown her on more than one occasion his priorities were elsewhere. He may not have always shown up when she wanted but he made it his business to be present when it mattered. Suki thought their anniversary was somewhere on that list, but his absence was proof she had been wrong. Very wrong.

Prepared to clean the mess, Suki slid her feet out of her heels, only to catch sight of her phone lighting up on the opposite side of the table. She had turned the ringer off so she could give Jinx her undivided attention tonight. The good that did her now. Annoyed, Suki's eyes rolled in her head. She was confident, Jinx finally decided to send a weak ass text to explain his absence. A text she had received on too many occasions. He'd make up an excuse, promise to make it up to her before either buying her an expensive piece of jewelry to add to her collection or send her on a trip, and if the offense was bad enough, he'd do both.

Walking the short distance, another message came through just as she reached to pick it up. When she didn't see the word *husbae* displayed across her screen, but an unsaved number instead, Suki's eyebrows knitted together as she clicked on the message, confused. No words were displayed, just two videos, causing Suki's eyebrows to dip further. Clicking on the first video, there was a lot of movement before the video finally came into view and Suki tried to make sense of what she was seeing on the screen.

"On the count of three... one, two, three!" the crowd screamed before pink confetti filled the air. *"Yasssss babe! I told you I was finally going to get my girl!"* the voice yelled before the video finally came into focus and a hollow feeling filled Suki's stomach. The video stopped just as the camera focused on a smiling Jinx holding the stomach of a stunning brown-skinned woman. Her teeth were perfect, and she looked so happy. With shaking hands, Suki exited the video before clicking on the second video.

The woman's face came into view again but this time, she was lying in a bed, her smile still on full display. She moved the camera around, showing her surroundings, and the sight before Suki caused tears to spring to her eyes. Suki clamped a hand over her mouth. The wine she had consumed threatened to come back up in a violent heave as her vision blurred. She wasn't sure if the sight of Jinx sleeping peacefully next to the woman was the cause of her sickness or the sight of the little mini versions of him lying across his chest were what shook her core.

A few seconds later, the video was back on the woman as she smiled triumphantly into the camera.

"Our little family is finally complete. Two boys and a girl," she spoke, hand rubbing her belly. *"Daddy was so happy; he finally gave me what I wanted."* She smiled, flashing her hand in front of the screen before the video ended.

The contents of Suki's stomach finally pushed past her fingers and spilled out all over the table. Her vision was blurred, and she didn't recognize the sound that escaped her lips. Suki had always heard of Jinx's infidelity. Sure, women approached her constantly about him. Everyone wanted Johnathan "Jinx" Bacalao, but she had him. Through all the allegations over the years, Suki held on to the fact that they wanted him, but he was hers and hers only; or so she thought. That illusion shattered as reality set in. Not only was there another woman, but she had his children. Not his child, but his *children*. Plural. More than one. So many thoughts swirled around in Suki's mind trying to figure out how this had become her life.

She had done everything right. She had saved herself for marriage. Jinx was the only man to ever have her body. Suki prided herself on being the perfect wife. Though she was young, she tried to be everything Jinx could ever want and more. Jinx had her by eight years in the age department, but Suki never saw it as an issue. Maybe that was the problem. Suki wasn't sure how old the woman in the video was, but she was certain she was older than her twenty-six years.

With tear-filled eyes, Suki took in her surroundings and suddenly the spacious house started to feel as if the walls were closing in on her. Her breathing became ragged and the only thing on Suki's mind was getting as far away from her home as possible. Rushing out of the living room and toward the staircase, she nearly tripped half a dozen times due to the wine in her system before she made it to the top. Suki pushed the door to the master bedroom open and went to her closet. She began frantically snatching articles of clothing from their resting places. She didn't have time to sort through and pick clothes, she just needed some things to hold her over until she could make it to the mall the next morning.

Once her small duffle bag was filled to her satisfaction, Suki snatched up the bag and made her way to her dresser. Sifting through the drawers, she pulled out a pair of stacked sweat pants. Taking off the robe, she didn't have time to change so she slid the bottoms over the teddy before finding a plain white t-shirt to throw on top. Realizing she was barefoot and hadn't packed any shoes, Suki raced back to the closet and grabbed the first pair of sneakers her eyes landed on. An off-white pair of Dior runners and a jean jacket. Sliding her sock-less feet into her shoes, she threw the jacket over her shoulders before walking back out to grab her duffle and purse. Whatever Suki didn't have, she would buy, but she had to get out of there before Jinx decided to show his face.

Prancing down the steps, Suki searched for where she had dropped her phone and once she located it, she walked out the door, only to be greeted by one of her husband's workers.

"Mrs. Bacalao, is everything okay?" Brick questioned with concern etched on his face.

Brick had never seen his boss's wife with a hair out of place, but here she was standing before him looking like a mad woman with mascara tears and smeared lipstick. His hand began to reach for his phone. He was positive his boss would want to know about his wife's disheveled appearance and strange behavior. Suki's eyes noticed his hand moving toward his pocket and instantly put up a hand to stop him.

"Everything is fine, Brick. There is no need to call Jonathan," Suki assured him. "Please call the car around so I can leave."

"But ma'am," Brick began.

"BRICK, DO AS I SAID!" Suki snapped.

She knew he was only doing his job, but his thoroughness was working against her at the moment. Suki knew without a doubt Brick would call her husband the first chance he got, but as long as she was off the Bacalao estate when it happened, she didn't give a fuck what he did.

"Yes ma'am," Brick told her before taking his radio off his hip and radioing down to the gate.

Suki anxiously bounced from one leg to the other waiting on her driver to make it to the door. If she was in any shape to do so, she would drive herself wherever she needed to go, but the alcohol she consumed and tears that wouldn't seem to stop falling let her know it wasn't happening.

A couple minutes later, Suki saw the headlights of the Maybach coming around the circular driveway. The driver came to a stop at the bottom of the steps, and when she saw him getting out to come open the door for her, she stopped him.

"It's fine, Clarence, I got it," Suki informed him, already making her way down the steps. She could tell he wanted to protest, but he gave her a simple nod instead. Once her driver was sure she was secured in the car, he looked at her through the rearview mirror, awaiting further instructions.

"Where to Mrs.?"

"The Ritz downtown," Suki replied.

Simply nodding, Clarence put the car in drive and headed to their destination. Suki allowed her head to rest against the seat as her mind roamed. She knew it was only a matter of time before Jinx found out her whereabouts. The workers may have loved her, but their loyalty would always be with the man who signed their checks. There would be no point in turning off her location because she knew he could find her. He had designed it that way from the day she said "I do." Putting a plan together in her mind, Suki knew she wouldn't be able to escape Jinx forever, but she had to buy herself some time until she was ready to see his face and hear his weak explanations. Suki wasn't sure when that would be, she just knew it wouldn't be tonight.

CHAPTER TWO

The sun on Jinx's face caused him to stir in bed. Opening one of his eyes, he closed it back instantly as his head pounded viciously. He could barely remember the night's events, but one thing was certain, he had a hangover. Feeling around in the bed, he realized no one was in the bed with him and groaned internally.

"Suk!" Jinx called out in a hoarse voice. "Suki, bring me a bottle of water and two aspirin, baby!"

A minute later, he heard the sound of feet hitting the floor and confusion swarmed his brain. Attempting to open his eyes again, Jinx struggled against the sunlight as his eyes tried to focus. Taking in his surroundings, Jinx realized he wasn't at home in his bed and dread instantly filled his heart. Checking the watch on his wrist, he realized it was after nine in the morning.

What the fuck? Jinx thought to himself, trying to sit up.

"Daddy!" he heard a little voice squeal. The hangover made the voice sound like nails on a chalk board, causing him to wince.

His eyes focused on his son Junior's smiling face.

Fuck, this is worse than I thought, Jinx cursed himself while smiling at his oldest.

"What's up, daddy's man?" Jinx greeted, ruffling the little boy's curly hair. "Where's ya mama?"

"Her in the kitchen feeding Melo panny cakes."

"Did you eat yours?"

"No Daddy. Mommy told me to come get you when her heard you yell," Junior replied.

"Oh really?" Jinx replied, "Well let's not keep Mommy and your tummy waiting. Let's go get you some pancakes."

"Okay Daddy!" Junior smiled before he jetted out the room and back down the hall.

Jinx smiled until Junior was out of sight, but on the inside he was fuming. Not only did Marina not wake him up last night, she was in the kitchen cooking as if he didn't stay out all night. The thought of being out all night caused Jinx to look around the bed for his phone, only to find it on the nightstand beside him completely dead.

"Fuck!" Jinx cursed under his breath.

Closing his eyes for a minute, his headache was instantly worse because his slip-up kept getting worse and worse by the second. Opening them again, Jinx checked his surroundings to make sure he had everything he needed before standing to his feet and following the aroma of food to the kitchen. Jinx's jaw flexed when he walked into the kitchen to see Marina humming away with a smile on her face as if his world wasn't crashing at his feet.

"Good morning, baby!" She smiled when she noticed his presence. "I just finished the eggs. Sit down and I'll fix your plate."

Jinx's eyebrow raised some in her direction, because why the fuck did she expect him to stay when she knew he couldn't? The smile on Marina's face was pissing him off because she was acting as if this was a normal routine for them. Walking over to his baby boy's high chair, he leaned down and kissed the top of his head while his syrup-stained face smiled up at him. Jinx had never planned on having kids with Marina, but here he was on his third. He didn't regret his seeds in the slightest, but they were a complication in his current life picture.

"Nah, I'm good," Jinx told Marina. "Let me holla at you in the living room for a minute."

Jinx walked away without waiting on her reply because he knew she'd be following him whether she wanted to or not. Jinx paced the small area waiting on her to join him. The moment she stepped around the corner where the kids could not see them, Jinx grabbed Marina's arm and forcefully pulled her toward him.

"What the fuck you got going on?" Jinx questioned in a hushed voice.

Marina could see the aggravation on his face, and that alone caused her to catch an attitude of her own.

"Nigga, is you crazy, let go of my fucking arm," Marina spoke, a little too loud for Jinx's liking. She tried to snatch her arm out of his grasp, causing him to grip it tighter.

His children had never witnessed them arguing and they wouldn't start today because their mama was on her bullshit.

"Lower your fucking voice," Jinx hissed.

"Let go of my arm, Jinx!" Marina growled but lowered her voice as he instructed.

Marina knew he would be pissed when he woke up without a doubt, but she didn't expect him to put his hands on her. Even if it was only snatching her up. Granted, Marina wasn't new to Jinx grabbing her forcefully or pushing her here and there while they argued, but he had never done so while she was pregnant.

Jinx's nostrils flared but he let her go with a slight push. His eyes went to her stomach, and he was pissed she was pregnant because he was ready to punch her in the fucking forehead.

"What is your problem?" Marina questioned.

Jinx's head whipped in her direction as his eyes narrowed.

"What's my problem?" Jinx repeated rhetorically. "What the fuck kind of question is that, Marina? But since you want to act fucking dumb, my problem is, I woke up in your bed with a dead phone instead of in my own with my *wife*."

"You fell asleep after the gender reveal and I didn't want to wake you," Marina explained lamely.

"Why the fuck not!"

Now it was Jinx's turn to raise his voice. Jinx knew he was pushing it attending Marina's gender reveal on the same night he had plans with Suki, but he felt he could swing it. He had been juggling the two women for years now and had yet to have any slip-ups before now. It had been easy because Marina had always known about Suki. She played her part and stayed out of the way, and Jinx had never given Suki any reason to question his fidelity. Yeah, Jinx may have had women coming at him constantly. He had even fucked more than a handful of them, but they never had any proof.

As crazy as it sounded, Jinx had a strict set of rules when it came to cheating. The number one rule on top of that list was no staying out overnight and always using condoms. He bought so many plan B pills for bitches, he was positive he may have been their number one customer. Marina had fallen through the cracks years ago and after a bad reaction she had to birth control, Jinx tried to be as careful as he could with her, but the damage was already done. He would rather have his kids with Marina than have multiple women running around with his heirs.

Marina had played her position perfectly and had never give him any reason to think she was on bullshit until now.

Marina's eyes rolled in the top of her head at the mention of Jinx's wife. She didn't need a reminder he was married. The ring on his finger was proof enough.

"You were tired and when I came in to wake you up, you and the boys were sleeping so peacefully so I left you alone. By then, I had fell asleep too."

Jinx face showed Marina he didn't believe one word she spoke, but what could he do to prove she was lying?

"I mean, it's not like she cared anyways because your phone didn't ring all night," Marina pointed out, pissing Jinx off more.

"That's probably due to the fact it's dead!" Jinx seethed. "Look, kiss the boys for me, I gotta go."

"You're not going to eat?"

"Fuck no, I'm not eating, Rina. I got to go home and pray I still have a house to come home to."

"You act as if Miss Goody Two Shoes is really built for that," Marina scoffed.

"Watch your mouth," Jinx warned. "I don't know if it's the pregnancy hormones or what, but you don't speak on my wife. Ever. You don't even speak her fucking name."

"I'm allowed to fuck her husband and have his kids, but I'm not allowed to speak her name? Nigga, get real," Marina told him with a roll of her eyes.

Jinx smirked to himself to hide his annoyance, because Marina's mouth almost made him forget she was carrying his daughter in her womb.

"Yeah, I see you in your feelings so I'ma leave, but don't forget what the fuck I said," Jinx spoke. "I may or may not see you later on this week." With that, Jinx turned and walked out of the living room.

Marina listened to him say his goodbyes to the boys before the door opened and closed, signaling his departure. Tears welled up in Marina's eyes, but she refused to let them fall. Jinx may have thought he had one up on her talking to her crazy, but Marina knew he would be back before he realized it. Jinx was so positive his wife would be home waiting on him. The videos Marina had her best friend send to Suki told Marina another story. If she was dumb enough to still be waiting on him after seeing them, Marina would just have to approach it a different way. But one way or another, Marina planned to have Jinx to herself by any means necessary.

———

Jinx broke damn near every traffic law known to man trying to cut down the hour drive from Marina's house to his estate by as much as possible. Jinx hadn't even bothered to put his phone on the charger on his drive because he didn't need to see all the hateful shit Suki sent to his phone. After a forty-five-minute drive, Jinx's estate came into view, and he released a breath he didn't know he was holding.

The guard outside the estate noticed him approaching and opened the gate, which Jinx almost hit with the front of his car because it wasn't opening fast enough for him. He drove up the driveway faster than normal and when he made it underneath the porte cochere, Jinx hopped out of his car and didn't bother turning off the engine as he raced up the steps and rushed into the house. He didn't even greet his doorman and bodyguard, Brick, on the way inside.

"Yo, Suki!" Jinx yelled into the empty area.

Only silence greeted him as he moved through the lower

level of the house in search of her. When he made it to the dining room area, he saw the mess left over from Suki's surprise and his heart dropped. The big number five balloon and small red balloons had Jinx instantly cursing himself. Jinx had completely forgotten their anniversary was yesterday. On top of all his other transgressions, forgetting about the day they exchanged vows had to be the worst yet. He knew the date was approaching but he had been so consumed with Marina's gender reveal, it slipped his mind. Jinx wondered for a second if that was the reason she had chosen to have it on that particular day but immediately pushed it to the back of his mind. If he couldn't remember his anniversary, there was no way Marina remembered. It had to be a coincidence.

"SUKI!" Jinx yelled out again. Turning on his heels, Jinx was prepared to look for her upstairs when Brick walking in with a somber look on his face stopped Jinx in his tracks.

"Where's Suki, Brick?" Jinx asked.

"I tried to call you last night, Mr. Bacalao," Brick started.

"Call me last night for what? Where is my wife?"

"She left about one this morning in a rush. She looked as though she had been crying."

"FUCK!" Jinx yelled. "My phone's dead, let me borrow your phone so I can call her."

"Ummm, that's the thing," Brick started, "Clarence dropped her off at a hotel downtown and he didn't realize until he got back she had left it in the backseat. He tried to take it back to where she had him drop her off, but they have no record of her checking in, sir. It seems she went somewhere else and there's no way for us to know where..."

Brick's voice trailed off as Jinx's heart started to beat in his ears. Jinx had thought of every possible thing that could go down when he walked in the house after being gone all night, but Suki leaving him was never a thought. Jinx cursed himself for his carelessness. Jinx may have had a problem keeping his dick in his pants and he had his fair share of secrets, but none of that took away from the fact that he loved his wife. Jinx wouldn't know what he would do if Suki tried to leave him for good. He didn't know where she had disappeared to, but she could only get so far without his money. Jinx was sure once she calmed down, she'd come home. Jinx was all she had, and he had made sure of it. She would come back. She had to.

CHAPTER THREE

THREE DAYS LATER...

Cheeko's thumb drummed against his knee to a tune only he could hear in his head. He had been waiting for the past ten minutes on the property manager for a building he was interested in buying to show up for their meeting. He had shown up twenty minutes early but after waiting, he was second guessing this decision. Cheeko was a very punctual man, and his time was money. To him, early was on time and on time was late. Cheeko needed people around him who understood that.

"She's late," Cheeko announced.

"Calm down, Cheek. Not everyone thinks the same way you do," his sister and accountant, Simone, reminded him.

Cheeko chose not to reply to her, instead allowing his eyes to roam his surroundings. The meeting place was at a lounge in what he assumed was a convenient location for both parties. The atmosphere was chill and the music they chose set a peaceful mood. Cheeko approved. Just as he was getting ready to turn his attention toward the figure approaching his table, a woman at the bar caught his eye.

It wasn't her face that caused Cheeko to look twice, it was her body language. Everyone seemed to be having a good time, either smiling or talking to someone, but not her. Her energy seemed sad, and she wasn't smiling, just staring into her drink. Cheeko could tell she had either been crying or was trying to keep herself from doing so.

"Good afternoon, Mr. Saint James. Sorry for my tardiness. Traffic was excruciating coming from my office, this time of day," a voice spoke.

Cheeko watched the woman at the bar for a few more seconds before turning his attention toward the voice. Standing in front of him was a slim, middle-aged white woman with shoulder-length brown hair and green eyes. Her face wasn't painted up underneath a ton of makeup, but the scent of her perfume overwhelmed Cheeko's senses. The smell was old fashioned and reminded him of an old white woman twice this woman's age.

"I haven't been waiting too long," Cheeko commented, gesturing for the woman to take a seat. "This is my accountant and younger sister, Simone St. James. I asked her to sit in on this meeting with us. She attends every meeting when my money is involved."

"I completely understand. Nice to meet you, Simone. My name is Brianna Brockton." He watched as the women shook hands before Brianna turned her attention back toward him. "I have to admit, I'm a little surprised by your appearance."

"How so?" Cheeko questioned with a raise of his eyebrow.

"I looked over the portfolio you sent over and I was impressed by all the successful businesses you have underneath your belt. I did some digging of my own and you have quite an impressive resume," Brianna gushed.

"I'm not seeing where this would raise surprise," Cheeko told her with a flat look on his face, causing Simone to clear her throat.

"I think what my brother means is, what about your findings made you surprised at his success?"

"I guess I wasn't expecting your appearance is all," Brianna answered. "There are no pictures of you whatsoever online. You're virtually a ghost."

"So, which part surprises you? The fact I'm young, or that I'm black?" Cheeko questioned.

Brianna's mouth opened and closed like a fish out of water as her eyes bounced back and forth between the siblings. Simone closed her eyes for a brief second before opening them and seeing Cheeko stand to his feet. Brianna's eyes followed his movements as he buttoned the front of his tuxedo jacket.

"If you'll excuse me," Cheeko announced. "Simone will get the numbers you are suggesting for the property you manage but before the deal is done, I'd prefer to speak to the actual owners. If the numbers pan out, let them know I will be in touch with them and them alone. Have a nice day, Ms. Brockton."

Cheeko didn't wait for her response before he walked away. Cheeko wasn't at all surprised by her reaction. He got it more times than he could count. It was the main reason he had chosen to keep his face off any of his websites. Christian "Cheeko" Saint James was a lot of things but dumb was not one of them. In the corporate world, he knew if people saw him before a meeting, his success wouldn't mean anything. They would only see a black man with dreads and tattoos. No matter how nice he dressed, how articulate he was, or how much money he had at his disposal, Cheeko would be seen as just another black man trying to fit into corporate America. In a world not his own.

Most people waited their turn to be invited to the table. Not Cheeko. He didn't need people to open doors for him and make room at the table. He was content with kicking them down and demanding a seat.

Allowing Simone to take the meeting was the smartest move Cheeko could make because he was very interested in the property. Brianna's biased behavior wasn't the only motivation for him to end the meeting early. The sad, beautiful woman at the bar was an equal force in his decision.

"Is this seat taken?" Cheeko questioned, standing next to the woman whose eyes had yet to leave her martini glass.

"Um, no," she replied, barely looking in his direction.

Unbuttoning his jacket, Cheeko pulled the chair out some so he could sit comfortably. Cheeko's fingers tapping against the bar caught Suki's attention, but she chose to ignore him. His cologne already had her crossing her legs at the ankle and his manicured fingers were a plus. Suki learned a long time ago she had a thing for well-groomed men, hence why she fell for Jinx in the first place. Only to learn he was a well-groomed dog. She didn't need to see this stranger's face to tell he was a dog too. All men were.

"Does me sitting here offend you?" Cheeko questioned randomly.

Cheeko watched the woman's nose wrinkle slightly at his presence, and the scowl that momentarily graced her face didn't sit right with him either. Cheeko studied the side of the woman's face. He could see the wheels spinning in her head, causing his own to do the same.

"Excuse me? What?" Suki questioned, still not giving Cheeko her eyes.

"Your body language changed when I sat down. If my presence is offending you in any way, I can find another seat."

"No. That's not it. Sorry."

Suki's apology came out in a mumble. She hadn't noticed her thoughts could be read so easily. Jinx was still finding a way to ruin her day and he wasn't even present.

"Then what is it exactly?" Cheeko pressed, his fingers still dancing across the bar top.

"Are you always this pushy with strangers in public places?" Suki huffed, finally turning toward the deep voice, who seemed particularly interested in her business.

Suki had to keep all her composure so her mouth wouldn't fall open and release the saliva she could feel accumulating in her jaws. She didn't want to describe him as beautiful, but any other word didn't quite fit. Jinx wasn't too shabby himself, but this man? He was model worthy. Like *GQ* cover worthy.

Cheeko smiled at the woman, causing his dimples to show just slightly underneath his low facial hair. The annoyance in her voice should have given Cheeko the clue she didn't want to be bothered, but being able to see her from this angle was worth his intrusion. He had made up in his mind on the walk over he would buy her a drink, if she ever finished the one she was babysitting. But now, seeing how breathtaking she was, he knew he had to push a little further than that.

"Am I being pushy?" Cheeko asked, with a small chuckle. "Just curious, I guess. But again, if I'm offending you, I can find another seat," Cheeko offered.

"Umm. No. It's not you," Suki explained. "Just having a bad day, I guess."

"Want to talk about it?"

Before Suki could answer, the bartender came over to take his drink order.

"And add whatever she's having to my tab."

"You don't have to do that," Suki spoke. "I've been sitting here with the same drink for over an hour. I thought a drink was what I needed but, as you see," Suki explained, gesturing toward her drink.

"Which brings me back to my question. Do you want to talk about it?"

"Why would I want to do that? I don't know you well enough to tell you anything about me," Suki pointed out.

A smooth chortle passed through Cheeko's lips, and he watched his fingers for a second before he gave her his eyes again.

"The same reason people pay to tell complete strangers their business day in and day out," Cheeko told her. "Therapy is a very profitable business from what I understand."

"So, you're a therapist?" Suki questioned, with a skeptical look on her face.

"No, not at all. Just a businessman." Cheeko laughed. "But I've been told I'm a good listener. Just think of it as a therapy session, free of charge. You're able to get whatever is bothering you off your chest and get a completely unbiased response. If you're looking for one, that is. If not, I can just listen."

"But why?"

For the first time since he sat down, Cheeko's fingers stopped tapping and he thought about her question. Whatever she was going through was none of his business and normally, he wouldn't have offered to listen to her problems. He had enough of his own. But there was something about her sad eyes that made Cheeko want to ease her pain. Even if only a little.

"You just look so sad," Cheeko admitted. "If me listening to you will ease some of that sadness, then I'm willing to do that."

Suki opened her mouth to reply, but someone approaching them stopped her words in her throat.

"Cheek, I'm about to head back to the office to push some numbers around," the woman announced.

Suki turned toward her and instantly saw the resemblance between her and the stranger sitting next to her. The woman was beautiful.

"Did you get the asking price?" Cheeko asked, turning his attention toward his sister.

"Yeah. I'm sure after they learned what happened today, we can get them to go down in price by at least five. Ten if they feel bad enough about their worker," Simone replied, her eyes finally falling on a curious Suki. "I'm sorry, I didn't realize you were talking to someone."

"Simone, this is..." Cheeko began but realized he hadn't asked her name.

"Suki. Suki Bacalao," Suki filled in, reaching a hand toward Simone's to shake.

"Bacalao, Bacalao," Simone repeated to herself as if she were thinking. "Wait, as in Bacalao Enterprises?"

"That's the one," Suki told her with a smile. She wasn't fond of speaking on her husband at the present, but Bacalao was a well-known name. From real estate to construction contracts, the Bacalao name was usually somewhere in the mix, so she wasn't surprised when someone recognized it.

"So, you're related to Jonathan Bacalao?"

"He's my husband," Suki replied, lifting her left hand and showing the 2.5-carat, pear-shaped, canary diamond wedding ring.

"Small world," Cheeko commented. He watched as Suki slightly cut her eyes in his direction at her revelation. He couldn't tell if his remark offended her or if she was trying to read him.

She may have thought his unreadable expression was due to learning she was unavailable, but it was the opposite. Her being married didn't matter to Cheeko one way or the other because her ring was the first thing he noticed when he sat down. Cheeko was more interested in the fact that her eyes were sad at her revelation than anything. Her face wore a small smile, but her eyes told a different story. When he got married, Cheeko wanted his wife to beam with pride when she spoke of their nuptials. Not look as if it were a ball and chain rather than a wedding ring.

"Definitely a small world," Simone gushed. "I was planning to call your office tomorrow about the meeting I just had with one of your employees, Ms. Brockton."

"Simone," Cheeko spoke, his voice a sort of warning. Simone was all about business. Most days, Cheeko welcomed it because she was a huge asset to his team, but she could also have tunnel vision at the wrong times. Like now.

"What?" Simone questioned, looking at her brother.

"I heard you mention something about her behavior when you first walked up," Suki told Simone. "How about you leave me the folder you have in your hand and a phone number I can reach you at and I'll look everything over tonight. I'll give you a call first thing tomorrow. I'm sure we can work something out that works for everyone. Sound good?"

"Sounds great," Simone squealed.

Cheeko shook his head at his sister's theatrics but didn't say anything as he sipped his drink and watched her hand Suki a card with her information on it along with the folder.

"Thank you so much, Mrs. Bacalao," Simone told her, smiling.

"Call me Suki."

"Suki," Simone repeated. "I'll let you two get back to your...conversation. It was nice meeting you Suki. Cheek, I'll see you later on."

Cheeko nodded his head at Simone's departure but could feel Suki's eyes on him.

"I'm guessing the free therapy session is off the table, huh?" Suki questioned with a shy smile, breaking the silence between them.

"Why is that?" Cheeko questioned, even though he knew the answer.

Suki held up her hand once again as if it was evidence enough.

"Small things to a giant, ma," Cheeko told her. "Small things."

———

"Story Time" by Fivio Foreign came through the speakers, serving as background noise as Cheeko's fingers swiftly moved through the bills in his hands. The money he was counting was supposed to be rubber banded and packed already, but he had stayed out longer than he had planned the night before. After Simone left the bar, he didn't expect things to go much further with Suki outside of finishing his drink at the bar, but he ended up spending most of his night with her.

They stayed at the bar talking until it was time to close and by then, it was too dark to allow her to walk back to her hotel room alone so he escorted her. Cheeko couldn't remember the last time he had just spent time talking to a female. Most of his conversations ended one of three ways, with his dick in a bitch's mouth, her pussy, or with him dismissing her and not seeing her fit to touch him at all. Call it what you will, but Cheeko was selective with his women. He had bougie dick and he wasn't ashamed in the slightest.

By the time Suki finally passed out from all the drinks she had consumed, it was well after three in the morning, giving

Cheeko the opportunity to slip out. He could have stayed and blamed his intoxication for the impromptu sleepover, but in the little time he had spent with Suki, he had developed a respect for her that wouldn't allow him to sleep comfortably. He never figured out what had her looking so sad, but he could bet money it had something to do with her husband. Even still, Cheeko could tell Suki wasn't looking to get her nigga back for whatever he had done. She just needed a friend, and in that moment he was willing to be that for her.

Leaving his number on the notepad that rested on the nightstand, Cheeko turned out the lights and eased out of the room, careful not to wake her. It took everything in him to keep his eyes open on the hour drive home but he made it there unscathed and passed out on arrival. Now here it was nearly eleven in the morning and running behind was an understatement. Only thing was, Cheeko had no regrets.

The sound of his buzzer going off pulled his eyes away from his task, but his fingers never stopped moving. Cheeko could count money in his sleep. His eyes landed on the screen to his left, it gave the perfect view of his front door allowing him to see who was on his doorstep, even though he already knew. Finishing his count, Cheeko stood up and went to let his guest inside.

"Damn man, what, you was in here beating ya meat or something? Took you long enough."

Cheeko didn't even bother responding to what Nahz said because his default button was always set to bullshit whenever he opened his mouth. Cheeko walked back to where he was sitting and put a rubber band on the stack he had set to the side, waiting on Nahz to join him.

"Man, I know you didn't have me ride all the way over here and the money not even together," Nahz complained. "Yeah, you definitely was in here beating ya meat."

"You gon' stand there and talk shit or are you going to help me get this shit together?" Cheeko questioned, his hands already busy again working on the pile of money.

"I'ma help but I still want an answer to my question."

"You didn't ask a question."

"I've known you since we were ten and I can count on one hand how many times you've been late doing some shit and nigga, I still have four fingers left."

"That's still not a question, Nahz," Cheeko pointed out in annoyance. "Either ask me what the fuck you gon' ask me or shut the fuck up so I can concentrate."

Nahz had been Cheeko's best friend since the fifth grade and in all that time, you would think Cheeko was used to his theatrics, but nope. Nahz could still get under his skin like the little brother he never had. Simone was Cheeko's only sibling and she didn't even annoy Cheeko as much as Nahz did.

"My question is why? We got to meet this nigga in less than two hours, the money not bagged, you sitting around in some sweats, and I'm pretty sure you ain't even had time to go through your pretty boy ass routine you do every fucking morning. So why, today of all days, is Mr. Punctual not on his A game?" Nahz questioned, his voice dripping with suspicion.

"What are you my fucking mother now?"

"You deflecting."

"Not that it's any of your fucking business, but I overslept," Cheeko told him, giving him a half truth.

It wasn't a complete lie because he did oversleep. Cheeko was just leaving out the fact that he made it home at the exact time his alarm was going off for him to get his day started.

"Bullshit," Nahz spoke, his eyes narrowing toward Cheeko.

"Nigga, either get to counting or get out. I'm already in a bad mood and I don't need you making me later than I already am to this fucking meeting you insisted we have."

Cheeko knew if they were late, it would be his own doing, but Nahz was pissing him off pointing out all the shit he was behind on.

"Yeah, yeah. Whatever. Go ahead and handle your business while I finish this up," Nahz told Cheeko. "Don't need you giving a nigga extra work because you didn't have time to exfoliate your patchy ass beard," Nahz joked.

"Coming from a motherfucka that can only grow a goatee," Cheeko joked back but stood to his feet to do exactly what Nahz suggested.

Just because Cheeko had been against the meeting initially, he was well aware he needed the guns from this guy Nahz had suggested they meet. One of Cheeko's clients was in need of a larger shipment than Cheeko currently had at his disposal, but one thing he never did was leave money on the table for someone else to take. Cheeko was a businessman through and through, and whether he was dressed in a suit walking into a boardroom meeting discussing expansion or getting his products off to the highest bidder, he was about his paper and his time was money.

Nahz laughed Cheeko off and continued to count the money. Nahz may have annoyed Cheeko to no end most of the time but he was grateful for him every day of the week. Swaggering off to his room, he checked the time on his phone and realized he needed to get moving if he wanted to keep his schedule. He also noticed Suki had yet to reach out to him, but he'd worry about her later. Cheeko wasn't patient with a lot of things, but he could be patient for her. Something was telling him she was worth it and much more, even if she didn't quite understand her worth just yet.

CHAPTER FOUR

Light knocking on her hotel room door pulled Suki from her slumber. Looking around the room, she tried to figure out where the knocking was coming from until she heard the noise again. Detangling herself from the pile of sheets, Suki stood to her feet, trying to make it to the door to catch the visitor before they left. No one outside of her visitor last night knew where she was staying, so she knew it had to be one of the hotel staff. But then again, Jinx's pull was long, and Suki knew it was only a matter of time before he tracked her down. She was running low on cash and if she wanted to stay away for any longer, she would have to cave and use one of her credit cards or make a stop at the bank to withdraw some money.

"Who is it?" Suki called out groggily.

"Room service."

Eyebrows dipping slightly, Suki checked to make sure she didn't have any dried-up slob on her face in the mirror next to the door before pulling the door open.

"I think there's been a mistake, I didn't order any room

service," Suki told the young lady standing in her hotel doorway.

"Um," the girl began, looking at a piece of paper that was in her hand. "Mrs. Suki, correct?"

"Yes, that's me," Suki confirmed.

"Then yes ma'am, this is for you." The girl smiled.

Stepping to the side, Suki allowed the girl to bring the cart inside. The aroma that passed her nose caused her stomach to rumble loudly, signaling she needed to feed herself. With all the liquor she consumed the night before, Suki knew the little lunch she had before walking down the block to the lounge had digested long ago.

"Hope you enjoy," the girl announced after setting everything up.

"Oh, let me grab my purse so I can tip you," Suki called out, eyes searching the room for her discarded bag.

"It's already been handled, ma'am." She smiled politely before heading toward the door.

Now Suki was really confused. Not only had she not ordered the food, she most definitely hadn't left a tip for anyone. Walking over to the cart, Suki's fingers touched the yellow roses that were placed there before bringing them to her nose and smelling them. A smile graced her lips. She had to admit the flowers were a nice touch and would thank the staff when she made her way downstairs. Ready to place the flowers back to where she got them from, a note sitting on the cart caught her attention. Picking it up, her smile grew wider as she read the words.

I wasn't sure what you liked so I picked a little of everything. Hope you like flowers and this don't come off as no stalker type of shit lol. Enjoy your day beautiful. Don't be afraid to use the number I left. -Cheeko.

P.S. Make sure you take the aspirin and drink the orange juice they brought up. You too pretty to be walking around with a hangover :)

Flipping the paper over, Suki didn't see a number attached to the note and wondered if he was mistaken. Deciding not to think too much into it, she sat down and began pulling the lids off the plates of food. Cheeko wasn't lying, he had thought of everything she may have liked. There was French toast, pancakes, blueberry muffins, scrambled eggs, a bowl of fruit, sausage, bacon, and regular toast. Along with milk, water, coffee, and orange juice. Picking up a strawberry and putting it in her mouth, Suki smiled at the gesture.

Suki had spent the last five years with Jinx, and she couldn't remember the last time he had done anything for her just because. Everything he did was either motivated by a fight they had gotten into or an apology for a fuck up. In a span of a couple hours, a complete stranger made her feel more seen than her own husband. Sighing at the thought, Suki sat down before she fixed herself a small plate. Settling on a muffin, some fruit, and orange juice, Suki took her time eating it, not wanting to overdo it. Spotting the aspirin, she heeded Cheeko's words and took them. She didn't quite feel the effects of a hangover just yet, but she'd rather be ahead of the game just in case one decided to sneak up on her later.

After finishing her breakfast, Suki decided to take a shower and handle the rest of her hygiene. She had a long day planned ahead and she was already behind. In her haste leaving her home days prior, she had only grabbed enough cash to last her two days max. She hadn't expected to stay gone for as long as she had, but she wasn't in the mood to hear any lame excuse Jinx had about missing their anniversary dinner. Or confronting him about the videos sent to her phone. Suki was still having a hard time swallowing that information. Out of all the time she spent with Jinx, kids weren't even an option for them, but now she understood why. He already had a family elsewhere.

A single tear came to Suki's eye at the thought, and she quickly swiped it away, not wanting to waste any more tears on the situation. Suki knew sooner or later she would have to deal with it, but a few more days of ignoring it wouldn't hurt anything. After she was dressed in one of the cute jogger and crop-top outfits she had picked up from the Target around the corner, Suki went back to the main room to have a look at the folder Cheeko's sister had left for her the night before.

Suki had stepped away from Bacalao Enterprises a year prior and had left Jinx to run the business how he saw fit, believing being a stay-at-home wife was the best option. But now, she realized she may have made a mistake. Suki had given up everything for Jinx to be a better wife. Her dreams of flipping houses, getting her degree, opening a shelter and community center for children, the whole nine, all for the sake of love.

The folder would give her something to focus on and Suki needed all the distractions she could currently get. Opening the folder, she looked over the proposal letter, the asking price, and the property and was impressed by its thoroughness. She wasn't exactly sure who had drafted the property information, but Suki could appreciate the dedication. After finding a few things in the document she wanted to change, Suki smiled because she had to admit she missed working.

Satisfied with what she had come up with, Suki looked for the card Simone had given her so she could make the call. Not seeing it in the folder, she remembered leaving it on the nightstand, when she and Cheeko made it to her room so she wouldn't lose it.

Walking over to the nightstand, Suki saw the card she was looking for, but scribbling on a piece of paper caught her attention. Seeing Cheeko's name along with a phone number on it caused Suki to smile yet again for what she felt was the hundredth time today. Suki felt she was on a roll with the smiling, and she knew once she got a new phone, she would find the time to text him. Even if it was just to thank him for the carefree night they shared along with him sending her breakfast. But at the present, Suki had business to handle, so Cheeko would have to wait.

Picking up the card instead, Suki sat on the edge of the bed before picking up the phone in the room and dialing the number. Listening to the phone trill on the other end, Suki was prepared to leave a message when the sound of panting came through on the other side.

"Simone St. James speaking."

"Hi, Simone. This is Suki," Suki began. "We met yesterday at—"

"Mrs. Bacalao!" Simone squealed in recognition. "Yes, I remember."

"Suki, please." Suki chuckled at her enthusiasm.

"Oh, right. Sorry," Simone told her with a chuckle of her own. "How can I help you?"

"I wanted to call you as I promised and let you know I was able to look over the folder you gave me. You did an impressive outline of the property and the things you planned to do with the building in your proposal."

"I wish I could take credit, but that was all my brother," Simone admitted. "He's very hands on when it comes to these types of things. I'm just the one who moves the money around and crunches the numbers."

"Really? Your brother doesn't seem like the type," Suki told her, meaning to say it more to herself than out loud.

When Simone chortled in her ear, Suki's face heated up with embarrassment.

"I'm sorry, I didn't mean it like that," Suki tried to explain.

"It's okay. I'm actually used to that reaction. My brother is a complex man, so I can understand how you got that impression from your initial meeting, but he's very passionate and a deep thinker. Especially with his projects."

"Well, as I said before, I can appreciate that," Suki told her.

Silence fell between the two before Suki cleared her throat, not wanting it to get awkward.

"But the reason I called was because I believe you are offering a fair price but in light of your incident, I wanted to offer you nine thousand from the original asking price."

"Wow, really?"

"Yes. I may not be as hands on as I used to be, but Bacalao Enterprises is just as much my baby as it is Jonathan's. Which means his employees are a reflection of me as well. I will make sure he is informed of her behavior but in the meantime, I believe this is the best way to correct the mistake. What do you say?"

"I say hell yes!" Simone exclaimed, causing Suki to laugh again. "Sorry, that was very unprofessional of me. But yes, that sounds great!"

"No worries!" Suki chortled softly. "I will make some calls into the office today so I can get the new proposal typed up for you to sign, and you should be able to drop the check off in a couple days. Does that work for you?"

"I have a better idea. How about you meet me at around three today and I can give you the check before you head to the office? That way, you're able to type up the new proposal but you won't have to wait on a check in the mail. Besides, I'd prefer to deal with you directly," Simone suggested.

"Um, I'm actually not dressed for the occasion," Suki told her, looking down at what she was wearing.

"Perfect, because neither am I. Today is my day off. We can meet for lunch and talk a little more. I'm sure we will be doing a lot more business together in the future so we can be serious then, but for now, we can just have a casual talk and get the small things ironed out."

Suki wasn't sure how she felt about meeting up in her current attire, but she respected Simone's business savvy attitude. She appreciated a woman about her business.

"Why not," Suki spoke, giving in. "Where do you want to meet?"

"There is this new Caribbean restaurant that just opened up downtown off Fifth Street, I've been dying to try."

"Sounds good. I haven't had Caribbean food in ages."

"Then it's a date," Simone beamed. "I'll see you at three."

"See you then," Suki replied, disconnecting the call.

Suki wasn't quite sure why she agreed to such an informal meeting, but she had to admit the prospect of getting food and drinks with someone other than herself was appealing. Even if it was with a complete stranger. Suki was two for two in the strangers department these days, but it beat staying in her room and sulking as she had done the past few days. Looking at the clock on the nightstand, she saw she had some time to relax and probably take a small nap before her not so formal business lunch date. Glancing over at Cheeko's number again, Suki made a mental note to stop by the phone store after their lunch to get a new phone. Falling back on the bed, Suki stared at the ceiling for a few seconds before closing her eyes. Yeah, a nap definitely wouldn't hurt anything.

———

Thanks to her Uber driver getting lost, Suki arrived at the restaurant ten minutes late. Since she didn't have a cellphone, she couldn't even text Simone to let her know she was going to be late.

Yeah. Leaving my phone was not the smartest thing I've ever done, Suki thought, chastising herself.

Walking into the semi-crowded restaurant, Suki walked over to the hostess stand.

"Hi. How many for you today?"

"Actually, I'm meeting someone. Last name St. James," Suki told the young black girl.

"Oh, yes. Your guest is already waiting on you. Right this way."

Suki offered her a smile before following her toward the back of the restaurant. As they approached the table, Simone's back was facing them, so she didn't notice them approaching.

"Can I get you something to drink?" the girl asked, as they made it to the table.

"Just an iced tea please," Suki told her, taking a seat.

Simone waited for the hostess to leave the table before she began talking.

"Hey girl. You look super cute," Simone complimented.

Suki had decided on a pair of light-wash, distressed jeans and a white Dior shirt to match the Dior runners on her feet. She threw a yellow cardigan over it and pulled her wild hair out of her face into a low, curly puff ball with her baby hairs laid. Her jewelry was modest, only sporting the Cuban link necklace she always wore, small hoops, and a watch. The necklace was her favorite 'I suck as a husband' gift from Jinx and her favorite piece of jewelry to date.

"Girl, I'm super dressed down," Suki told her with a wave of her hand.

"Honey, if this is dressed down, I can't wait to see you when you think you're dressed up," Simone commented, taking a sip of her water.

Suki smiled at the compliment.

"Sorry for being late, my Uber driver got lost. Apparently this place isn't on the map yet. Literally." Suki chuckled.

"It's okay, I actually just got seated maybe a minute or so before you walked up," Simone informed her. "I'm used to being the one late to everything and that usually causes an argument because my brother is the most punctual man on the planet," Simone told her with a roll of her eyes.

Suki chose not to reply but instead taking the initiative to look at her menu. The mention of Cheeko brought a small smile to Suki's lips that Simone noticed.

"Did I miss something after I left you and my brother at the bar yesterday?" Simone asked, bursting into Suki's thoughts.

"Huh?"

"Did something happen with my brother yesterday?" Simone questioned for more clarity.

Simone was very outspoken; it was just a part of her personality. Simone was also observant but at the same time, she knew her brother and knowing him, he had done something. From the look on Suki's face, Simone could tell he hadn't left a bad impression, but one could never be sure when it came to Cheeko. He was better handled in doses if you didn't know how to take him and his mouth.

"Uh, no," Suki replied. "I mean, not necessarily..." Her voice trailed off, just as the waitress returned to bring her drink.

"Are you ladies ready to order or would you like a few more minutes to look at the menu?"

"We're ready," both ladies answered at the same time.

Using the waitress as a distraction, Suki ordered her food, handing the waitress her menu once done, and waited patiently on Simone to order hers. Suki let her eyes roam the restaurant as her thoughts followed suit. The atmosphere was nice, but Suki was more concerned how to explain to Simone nothing was going on with her and her brother. But

Suki had to admit she wanted there to be something there, even if they were only friends. Cheeko was refreshing and Suki wouldn't mind having him around. How could there be though? She was a married woman. Jinx may have been a piece of shit, but it wasn't in Suki's behavior to step out on her husband.

Maybe Jinx deserved it, but Suki wasn't sure she could be the one to give his due justice. Besides, Cheeko was essentially a stranger to her. A handsome stranger, but a stranger all the same. Simone handed the waitress her menu and took a second to take Suki in. She could see her eyebrows furrowed ever so slightly while she stared off into space, unconsciously twirling her ring around on her finger where it rested. Simone wasn't sure what had her with such a faraway look in her eye, but now she was even more curious about what had transpired between this beauty and her brother.

"Uhem," Simone cleared her throat, catching Suki's attention.

Suki's cheeks warmed as she gave her attention back to Simone, realizing she had allowed her thoughts to get away from her.

"Sorry," Suki apologized.

"What for?"

"It's easy to get wrapped in my thoughts sometimes," Suki admitted.

"I'm sure that happens to the best of us," Simone told her, waving her off. "So..." Simone started, allowing her voice to trail off.

She may have given Suki a second to get her thoughts together, but she hadn't let go of the subject at hand.

"Oh, right," Suki told her. "But nothing happened honestly, other than us sharing a few drinks together before going back to my hotel room," Suki told her with a shrug.

The wide eyes and shocked look on Simone's face had Suki seeing she had made a mistake with her vague description.

"No, no. Nothing happened," Suki told her, chuckling softly at the instant relief that settled on Simone's face. "We actually spent the night talking. By the time the drinks finally caught up to me, the sun was just hours from peeking through the window. I must've fallen asleep because when I woke up, he was gone."

"Well, that's rude," Simone replied, kissing her teeth.

Cheeko may have been brash, but she knew he knew better than that. He could've woken her up at least and told her he was leaving.

"Not really," Suki defended. "It was the complete opposite."

Simone didn't reply but instead waited on her to elaborate on what she meant.

"On his way out of the hotel, he stopped and ordered me room service along with flowers and even paid for it. I tried to tip the girl and she waved me off and told me it had already been taken care of before she left. He may have left without telling me, but he still cared enough to make sure I would be well fed and wouldn't be battling a hangover all day. Your parents raised him right," Suki told her before taking a sip of her drink.

The entire time Suki recounted the events of the night before, a small smile graced her lips. Cheeko had left a lasting impression on Suki, and it was obvious.

"Yes, they did," Simone agreed but didn't press any further. Suki noticed she was allowing herself to get wrapped in her thoughts again and flashed Simone an embarrassed smile.

The waitress came over with their food, allowing the ladies to change gears of the conversation. They chatted over their meal, handling the business that had brought them together in the first place. The conversation flowed so freely between the two, Suki would bet her last dollar she had just made a friend. Jinx kept Suki under lock and key their whole relationship and most of their marriage. When she worked at the office, she was friendly with a few of the workers, but Suki wouldn't consider them her friends. She was their boss, the woman who signed their checks, so of course they were nice to her. Suki had always assumed Jinx's reasoning behind not wanting her out with friends and running the streets was his love for her and wanting her to act as a wife should. Now learning of his double life, she couldn't help but wonder if that was the only reason.

Simone's phone chiming cut into their conversation, causing Simone to glance at the screen before she groaned softly.

"I completely forgot I had somewhere else to be after this," Simone spoke. "Time completely got away from me and now I have less than an hour to make it across town."

"Oh, I'm sorry. I didn't mean to keep you."

"Girl, do not apologize." Simone waved her off. "I got business handled, got some good food and conversation out of the deal. I am not mad in the slightest. If it wasn't for this particular client, I would be finding a reason to hang out a little bit longer."

The way she said the word client stuck out to Suki, but she decided it wasn't her place to speak on it. She couldn't tell if Simone was excited or annoyed by the meeting, but it wasn't her business.

Simone reached across the table to grab the checkbook so she could handle the bill on her way out. After all, she was the one who had invited Suki out in the first place.

"Oh, you don't have to do that. Allow me to take care of it," Suki told her as she watched Simone sift through her handbag.

"Are you sure? I was the one who invited you out."

"True, but you're technically my client now," Suki explained. "So, allow me to handle it."

"Thanks girl," Simone told her. "Let me get out of here, and hit me up sometime. You have my personal number. I enjoyed myself, so we can do this again without the business hanging over my head. Maybe even go dancing or something."

Suki could feel the smile spread across her face before she spoke, "I'd like that."

"Cool! Talk to you later."

Suki waved as Simone rushed out of the building. She took another sip of her water before gathering her items and walking toward the front to the cashier booth. The young man smiled at her before holding his hand out for the leather folder.

"Did everything meet your standards?" he questioned as he looked down to his register and pressed a few buttons.

"Yes, everything was delicious, thank you. I will be coming back very soon," Suki told him while unzipping her purse and retrieving her credit card.

He took it from her and swiped it to handle the bill. When his eyes dipped, Suki watched him with curiosity, watching him try to swipe the card again.

"I'm sorry miss, but this card was declined," he spoke. "Would you like to try a different one?"

"Excuse me?" Now it was Suki's turn to furrow her brows. "Could you try it again?"

"I've tried it twice already," he told her with a small look of disdain.

"Just try it again, please," Suki pleaded with a small smile, glancing over her shoulder. A line was beginning to form behind her, and she knew she was holding everyone up.

Suki watched as he tried the card two more times before rolling his eyes back up to her face, his now masked in annoyance.

"The charge still did not go through, ma'am," he told her, completely annoyed having her waste his time.

"I'm sorry, I'm not sure what the problem is," Suki told him. Her hand shook slightly as she reached for the card the young man was extending toward her.

Suki had never been in a situation where her card declined, and she was beyond embarrassed. Not only was the cashier looking at her as if she was a bum, but the groans of the others waiting behind her were causing the hairs on the back of her neck to stand up.

"Would you like to try another card ma'am, or would you like to handle this with cash? There are others waiting."

Tears stung her eyes as they misted.

"Um, I can handle it with cash," she mumbled, peeling the money out of her wallet before placing the crisp bills into his outstretched hand. "Thank you," Suki told him before turning on her heels with her head down and rushing out of the establishment.

She could hear the murmurs of the patrons as the man called after her, most likely trying to give her the change. The moment she stepped on the sidewalk, cool air hit her face as she allowed her eyes to sweep the street. Spotting an ATM on the corner, Suki tried not to cause too much attention to herself as she made her way over to it.

Waiting patiently for the person in front of her to finish, she offered them a smile as they pulled their money from the machine and walked away. Suki had to take a few deep breaths as she tried to feed her card to the machine. Her nerves were shot because the card she had tried to use had an unlimited spending limit on it so it being declined had shaken Suki to her core.

Suki followed the prompts on the small screen but the moment she tried to move passed entering the pin, an error code popped on the screen telling her the account was no longer active. Retyping the information in twice more, Suki received the same message before a sinking feeling filled her stomach. Realization slammed into her like a ton of bricks. Jinx had taken her name from his account. Suki had three more cards in her possession, but she was positive she would receive the same results. The cards tucked safely in her wallet were no more valuable than plastic. Jinx had cut her off.

CHAPTER FIVE

The anger rolling from Jinx's shoulders could be felt in the cramped space. Suki had been gone for six days now and the longer she was gone, the angrier Jinx became. Not only had she been gone but she didn't show any signs of popping up any time soon. True, he had fucked up by skipping out on their anniversary dinner, but now Suki was taking things to the extreme.

Suki's credit cards hadn't been accessed at all in the time she had been gone and the thought had Jinx's jaw flexing. He needed her to come back home and the longer he waited, the need for her to forgive him was replaced with wanting to punish her for the grief she was causing him.

Jinx checked his watch as he sat in the backseat, ten minutes from his destination. He was being chauffeured by Brick because the way his mind was set up, he'd most likely crash into an unsuspecting car. That's just how distracted Suki had him. Jinx sat brewing in his anger as the car came to a stop, alerting him that he had made it to his meeting. Clearing his throat, he had to push all thoughts of his wife to the side to conduct business. Brick came around and opened the door for Jinx so he could get out of the car where two men were waiting on him.

At least these motherfuckers know how to be on time, Jinx thought.

Jinx allowed his eyes behind his shades to travel over the two men he was approaching, taking his time swaggering to where they stood. Both men were close to his height, one being slightly taller with his dreads pulled on top of his head and tattoos decorating his skin. While the other sported a low taper fade and a goatee. He could tell they were younger than him, which caused Jinx to smile on the inside. Young motherfuckers were willing to take any deal you gave them if you knew how to make the offer seem too good to be true. Jinx could practically see the dollar signs dancing behind his eyes.

Stopping just short of where they stood, Jinx took his shades off and placed them on top of his head before he began to speak.

"Gentlemen," Jinx greeted, his eyes bouncing between both men.

"You're late," the one with dreads spoke, causing the smile Jinx was sporting to fall from his lips slightly.

"Excuse me?" Jinx questioned.

"I said, you're late," he repeated, his face sporting an unmoved expression.

"Yeah, my apologies," Jinx offered. "West Coast traffic," he said, as if that was all the explanation he owed. "The name's Jinx."

"Cheeko," he replied. "And this is Nahz," the dread head spoke, nudging his head in the direction of the man standing next to him.

Jinx stared Cheeko down and instantly decided, he didn't like him or his attitude. He wasn't sure if it was the look on his face or his attitude, but Jinx could tell Cheeko felt he was better than him.

"Nice to meet you both."

"Likewise." Cheeko nodded.

Cheeko wasn't sure what it was about the man standing in front of him but from the moment he stepped out of the car and approached them, he knew he didn't like him. Not only was he late to a meeting he set up, but Cheeko could see it in his eyes once he lifted his glasses, Jinx was a snake. The man hadn't said more than a handful of words to Cheeko, and he had already rubbed him the wrong way. If Cheeko wasn't in need of the guns Jinx had, he would have left him where he stood. Jinx hadn't offered them a handshake and gave excuses instead of just admitting he had fucked up wasting their time. Both were immediate red flags in his eyes. Yeah, something about him wasn't right.

"Not to be rude, but I have a very tight schedule I need to maintain..." Cheeko started but let his words trail off so Jinx could see where he was headed with the conversation. Cheeko heard the low chuckle Nahz passed through his lips but chose not to speak on it.

"Ah, yes," Jinx told him. "I was informed you were in need of guns. Any specific kind you're interested in?"

"My client is looking to get their hands on anything from handguns to military grade weapons. As long as the guns are semi-automatic to fully automatic, the type does not truly matter. Though out of the selection, I would prefer you focus mainly on Berettas for the handguns, AK-47s, AR-15s, and G18s. Uzis need to be in the mix as well as an assortment of M24s, M21s, an SR-25, and at least ten AS-50s," Cheeko informed him, rattling off the names of the guns with ease.

"Your client, huh?" Jinx questioned. "So, that makes you

what? The middle man? If your client needed all of these guns, why not come to me directly to talk business?"

Cheeko's jaw ticked at being called a middle man, but he had to remind himself, the man standing in front of him didn't know him enough to realize his question was seen as disrespect. Cheeko wasn't a middle man of anything, but he was a bridge when need be.

"No, I'm not a middle man," Cheeko replied flatly. "I'm a courier of sorts. As I said, this person is *my* client. I need the guns. You have them. It's simple mathematics in my eyes. Where or who I sell the guns to once I leave here should not be any of your concern. If I decided to take all of them out on a boat to the middle of the Gulf of Mexico and dump them, it shouldn't concern you. The only concern of the deal between or business with me and my client, should stop once you get your money. My business is my business. Yours is yours. Now the question is, can you get the guns or not? If the answer is no, I will find someone who can."

Jinx watched the man standing in front of him, and blowing his brains out would satisfy Jinx's need to let off some frustrations, but he was not here for that. What Cheeko had said was true. Once the money was in Jinx's hands, he didn't give a fuck what Cheeko did with the guns. He had only asked the question to see how Cheeko would react. He wanted to know the depth of the man standing in front of him. Jinx had tried to do some digging when he was first approached about the meeting, but everything concerning the two men in front of him was a complete mystery. It was as if they didn't exist.

A smile spread across Jinx's face as he tried to ease the tension in the air.

"I apologize if I have offended you. I wanted to make sure I wasn't dealing with an amateur."

"Make it up to me by answering my question and telling

me if you have or can get what I need," Cheeko replied, not wavering in his stance.

"Yes, but it will take me two days to gather everything you requested. The ticket is two million," Jinx told him, throwing the number out.

"That's fine," Cheeko replied without flinching. He finally looked over at Nahz, who had been down toward the two duffle bags at his feet, unzipping both and removing money from one bag and placing it in the other.

Jinx watched the movements until Nahz zipped back up the bag he was taking the money out of and stood before walking over to Jinx and extending it in his direction. Brick stepped up and took the outstretched bag instead.

"That's five hundred thousand. You will get the rest once the guns are in my possession," Cheeko told him. "You can have someone call Nahz with a pickup time. You gentlemen have a good day."

Jinx watched as the men walked off carrying the heavier bag of money before sliding his shades back over his eyes. He didn't show it on his face, but on the inside Jinx was fuming. He would get Cheeko the guns he needed so he wouldn't have to deal with him again. Jinx had a feeling that if he had to lay eyes on the man again outside of business, it wouldn't end well.

———

"Oouuuuu! Fuuccccccckkk! Yessss, right there!" Moans filled the room along with the sound of wet skin smacking together.

Simone's eyes were nearly in the back of her head with her face planted in the pillow trying to take the back shots she was receiving. The constant thump against her G-spot had her mouth wide open. She knew she probably had drool dripping out the side of her mouth, but she didn't care. Feeling the familiar buildup in the bottom of her stomach, Simone tried to get loose from the hold she was in. Trying to find any way to stop the pressure, even if she knew her release was inevitable.

"Ahnt, ahnt, where you going Simone? I thought you wanted me to hit this spot right here?" her assailant taunted.

He watched the jiggle of her ass cheeks against his thighs while his hand kept her arms pinned against her lower back. Removing the hand he had guiding her backward onto his hard dick, he tangled his fingers into her hair before pulling her body up against his. Slowing down his movements some, he licked the side of her neck as his dick rubbed against the bundle of nerves inside her walls. Simone was choking his dick ever so slightly and it was driving him crazy.

Simone wanted to cry. Not from the subtle pain she was receiving but the immense amount of pleasure he was delivering to her. Simone tried to move her hips back to meet his thrusts, causing a smooth chuckle to pass through his lips. He knew with the grip he had on her, she wasn't going anywhere. She couldn't make him go any faster or any slower. This was his show and she'd take his dick in whatever way he chose to deliver it to her.

"What you trying to do? I'm not fucking you good enough?" he questioned, his hips never losing their pace. Her movements didn't bother him in the slightest as he rocked his hips, digger deeper, but never stopping his assault against her spot.

"I could always stop," he suggested, beginning to withdraw from her tight folds.

A whimper escaped Simone's lips at the sudden fullness leaving her.

"Please," Simone squirmed, clenching her walls attempting to prevent his exit.

Her walls gripping him caused him to close his eyes as a groan rumbled in his throat.

"Please, what?"

Simone didn't answer him as she pushed back, trying to sit back down on his dick, wiggling her hips, but he kept her at bay. Not liking her silence, he pulled another inch out.

"Nooooo," Simone cried out.

She was so close to her release, and he was moving it further and further away. Simone knew what he wanted. What he needed. It was always the same with them. This constant tug of war of who would dominate who. She always put up a good fight only to lose in the end. The control he had over her body drove her insane, but she couldn't get enough of him. Simone was addicted.

"Tell me," he spoke, continuing his withdrawal until only the tip of his erection remained.

"Ughhhh, fine," Simone whined. "Fuck me harder. Make me cum."

"What's the magic words?"

"Fuck you!" Simone snapped, tired of playing his game.

Laughing, he pushed Simone back forward, never letting go of the tight grip he had on her hair. Letting her arms loose, he smacked her ass hard, leaving a red handprint in his wake.

"Arch it," he demanded. "And you better not run," he warned, the aggression in his voice causing Simone's walls to leak.

Once she was how he wanted, he lifted one leg and planted his foot on the mattress before slamming back into her. Simone immediately tried to get out of his hold, but it was pointless.

A mixture of her moans and whimpers and his groans surrounded them as he tried to plant himself deeper in her walls. Her walls began to leak her arousal as her juices spilled out of her. Simone could feel the swelling of his dick alerting her that he was close to his release, causing her own to come to the forefront.

"Arghhhh, I'm about to cummmmm!" Simone cried out.

"Me too, bae. Let me have all that shit!" he growled, hitting her spot repeatedly.

As if his wish was her command, her orgasm ripped through her body, leaking all over his lower stomach and sheets. Panting replaced their moans as his dick twitched inside her, leaving his seed coating her walls. Slowly adjusting his angle, he allowed his head to fall on her back as he attempted to catch his breath.

A minute passed before Simone began to squirm in his hold, their bodies still connected.

"I know you didn't just nut inside me again, Nahzir!" Simone snapped, trying to push her hips back to knock him from inside her.

"Mannnn, stop moving for you break my dick off," Nahz mumbled against her skin with his eyes closed. "You know a nigga dick sensitive, and I can't feel my legs."

"I don't care! Get off me so I can go try to pee it out before it's too late!"

Instead of arguing with her, Nahz withdrew completely from her and rolled onto his bed with his eyes opening slowly. He watched Simone try to jump out of his bed only for her knees to get weak. Amusement danced in his eyes with a smile tugging the corner of his lips as she tried to make it to his attached bathroom before her legs gave out. She resembled a newborn deer and the thought caused Nahz to laugh lowly.

"It's not funny, Nahzir!" Simone yelled, slamming the bathroom door behind her.

Nahzir only shook his head as he looked around the room spotting her things scattered about. Not only were her discarded clothes on his floor but things she had left over time were in his space. Over the past six months, she had taken his home away from home and added her feminine touch. Things Nahz never thought about having were preoccupying his space. The books she read were on a coffee table she insisted he buy, along with decorative pillows to 'give the space more life' as she called it. When he first bought the condo, it was simply to have a getaway from his everyday life. Nothing permanent. Just somewhere he could crash when things got too hectic for him. It was just supposed to be a place of peace. Now, it was their place to creep.

Nahz listened to the water from the sink turn off before the bathroom door opened again. He allowed his head to fall against the mattress as his eyes found Simone's annoyed ones. Even with a scowl on her face, Simone was the sexiest woman Nahz had ever laid eyes on. Her cinnamon-colored skin and slender hips drove him crazy, but his favorite part of her body had to be her doe eyes. They were deep brown and so expressive. Anything she left unspoken, he could look in her eyes and have all the answers. They mirrored her soul.

"Say whatever you gotta say, Mone, instead of giving a nigga the death stare," Nahz told her, already knowing where the conversation was headed.

"Why would you nut in me? Again?"

"If you don't want me nutting in you, tell your pussy to stop choking my mans out," Nahz chuckled, sitting up in the bed.

Simone's eyes followed his movements, her eyes temporarily traveling to his flaccid penis. Even on soft, his size was impressive resting against his thigh, her essence still coating it. Simone tore her eyes away once she felt her clit thump.

"I'm serious, Nahzir," Simone whined. "What happens if I get pregnant? Then what?"

"Then we just going to have a little Nahz running around," he told her with a shrug as if the answer was that simple.

"I'm serious, Nahz."

"So am I," he stated, cutting his eyes at her. "If you so worried about getting pregnant, get on birth control."

"I told you already birth control isn't good for women's bodies. You can simply wear a condom."

"And I told you already, condoms aren't good for a nigga's dick," he rebutted.

"Why is everything a joke to you?" Simone asked, annoyance dripping in her tone. "I'm trying to have a serious conversation with you because if you don't start wearing condoms or learn to pull out, I will eventually end up pregnant. Then Cheeko is going to know everything."

"We're not hiding from Cheeko because of me. Remember that."

"You're not the least bit worried about his reaction? I'm his little sister and you're his best friend, Nahzir."

Granted, fucking his right-hand man's sister wasn't ideal, but the damage was done now.

"Why would I be worried? I'm a grown ass man, Simone. Don't no motherfucker worry me," Nahz told her, looking directly into her eyes.

Blowing out a breath in frustration, Simone rolled her eyes.

"All I'm saying is, me getting pregnant is the worst way for him to find out."

"Then let's call him and tell him," Nahz challenged, standing up. Panic set in when Simone watched him lean over to his discarded jeans in search of his phone.

"NO!"

Her voice caused Nahz to stop his movements as his eyes came back to her with a deep scowl on his face.

"No, what?"

When she didn't answer, Nahz crossed his room, his long strides causing him to make it over to her in no time. Simone bounced from one foot to the next, afraid to bring her eyes up to meet his menacing ones.

"No what, Simone?" Nahz questioned again, his voice low.

He watched her twist her hands together, a sign she was nervous, as she looked down.

"Not now," Simone mumbled.

Putting his finger under her chin, he brought her face in his direction, forcing her to look at him.

"Then when?" Nahz challenged.

"I don't know, Nahz, but not now. It's not the right time," Simone explained lamely.

Nahz's jaw ticked and his normally light-brown eyes began to darken as he stared down at her.

"It's never the right time," Nahz scoffed, dropping his hand and taking a couple steps away from her. "If I didn't know any better Simone, I'd think you were content with a nigga only being able to show you affection behind closed doors. What, you so scared of what your brother might say that you'd reduce yourself to a few orgasms after getting your back broke in and letting me nut in every hole on your body? Your brother's opinion is worth that much to you?"

"That's not fair!" Simone argued, taking a step in his direction.

"To who? You?" Nahz asked. "This whole situation is fair to you, Simone!" Nahz bellowed. "I'm a grown ass man sneaking around behind closed doors for your sake, not mine. Difference between me and you is, I don't give a fuck what your brother has to say! Either he gets with it or he got a problem with it, but the outcome can only go one or two ways. And I'm supposed to be the nigga that you love."

"I do love you, Nahzir," Simone told him.

"Then call Cheeko and tell him the truth. Tell him for the past two years we been fucking around behind his back."

"I can't," Simone whispered, her eyes falling away from his again.

"That's what I thought," Nahz told her. "I don't know why I thought this time would be different. If this is your version of love, shorty, I don't think I want it."

At hearing his words, Simone's eyes snapped back toward his.

"What are you trying to say?"

"I think I just said it," he told her with a shake of his head. His face was placid, but his eyes told a different story. Hurt echoed loudly inside them and Simone's heart sank. She knew she was the cause of his pain, and she wanted nothing more than to take it away.

"Nahzir," Simone called out lowly, reaching her hand out to touch him only for him to take another step back, causing her hand to fall short.

"I gotta take a shower so I can make some plays. You can let yourself out," Nahz told her in a low voice.

Stepping around her, Nahz walked into the bathroom closing the door behind him. When Simone heard the door lock, her heart broke a little more, feeling as if he was locking her off from his heart as well. Nahz just didn't understand the position he was placing her in. Yes, she loved him, but she loved her brother even more. Simone didn't want to be the reason for the discord. Nahz was the only friend Cheeko had and she knew their revelation could be the end of that.

How could Nahz ask her to carry that burden on her shoulders? Going around the room, Simone picked up her particles of clothing and slipped them over her body before putting on her shoes. Grabbing her purse and keys, Simone looked at the bathroom door once more before heading toward the front door to let herself out just as Nahz had instructed. Simone couldn't help but wonder if this would be the last time she walked through these doors.

CHAPTER SIX

The sight of her home's front gates coming into view caused immediate aggravation to settle in Suki's bones. She had chosen to stay away an extra two days after the restaurant fiasco but now with only thirty bucks to her name, Suki had no choice but to come back to the home she shared with her husband.

Just the thought of Jinx caused Suki to roll her eyes. She wasn't sure what she would do once she saw him, but she'd be lying if she said she didn't miss being in her own bed. Her Jacuzzi tub was screaming her name at this point and she couldn't wait to soak all the tension from her body. Pulling up to the gate, she had the driver roll her window down so the guard would allow her access to her own home.

"Hey Chad," was all Suki offered at the big burly white guy in front of her.

"Mrs. Bacalao. Nice to see you ma'am. I will alert Mr. Bacalao so he can meet you at the front door."

"No need, Chad. I'll see him once I make it inside."

"Yes ma'am," Chad responded, giving her a stiff nod before pressing a button to open the gate.

Hearing that Jinx was indeed home caused Suki's aggravation to get worse, but she had been expecting as much. The sun was setting outside so him being home wasn't out of the norm.

When he wasn't out creeping with his side bitch, that is, Suki thought with another roll of her eyes.

"Thank you," Suki told the driver who had come to a stop as she opened the back door.

The moment Brick's eyes landed on her, he sprang into action to meet her at the bottom of the steps.

"Mrs. Bacalao."

"I have a few bags in the trunk. Can you bring them inside for me and take them upstairs to one of the guest bedrooms? And please tip the driver."

"Yes ma'am," he told her with a slight nod before going to do as she asked.

Jinx may have forced Suki to come back home by cutting off her access to his money, but she would do so on her terms. She barely wanted to be in the same house as her husband. Sharing the same bed would be pushing it and Suki was not trying to be featured on an episode of *Snapped*!

Stepping over the threshold, the familiar smell of warm vanilla greeted her nostrils.

A scent she had placed all over the massive house. Yes, it was good to be home.

Suki closed her eyes for a moment, taking in the atmosphere. Being away for a week, Suki realized how quiet their home was. No laughter filled her halls. No little pitter patter of tiny feet to meet her at the door. The house smelled of one of love but felt cold and empty.

Hearing movement at the top of the staircase, Suki opened her eyes and began to head in the direction of the noise.

Might as well get this over with now.

"Brick, have Clarence bring..." Jinx's words trailed off as the sight of Suki greeted him.

His eyes roamed her body in the tight-fitting, one-piece black jumpsuit she had on. Her wild hair was untamed in a mass of curls framing her face. The black hair a contrast to her light skin.

"Suki," was all Jinx could say.

After she had been gone for so long, Jinx thought the attitude she had would have been gone by now, but the evil eye she was giving him told him otherwise.

Instead of responding to his presence, Suki made her way up the stairs. She could smell his cologne from where she stood, and the clothes that draped his body let her know he was on his way out. The thought of him going to see *her* and his children plagued Suki's mind, putting her in a dark space almost instantly.

Walking past where he stood, Suki turned in the opposite direction of their bedroom and headed toward the guest wing. The house consisted of seven bedrooms. Each of the bedrooms having a full en suite bathroom except two. Four of the guest rooms were upstairs and three were downstairs. Jinx's eyebrows dipped inward as he watched her turn the corner down the hall headed toward the guest bedrooms.

"SUKI!" Jinx called out to her as she rounded the corner.

Suki saw no point in turning around because from the sound of the aggressive footsteps behind her, she knew he was following her. Pushing the door open to the last bedroom in the hall, Suki flipped on the lights and was greeted with the lilac paint that coated the walls. The bed wasn't made but she'd get Brick or one of the other attendants who frequented the grounds to bring her what she needed up from the laundry room. Suki didn't close the room door but walked further in and placed her handbag on the unmade mattress before taking off her jean jacket.

"This don't look like our bedroom," Jinx's voice stated behind her.

"That's because it's not our bedroom. It's a guest room," Suki told him matter of factly.

"Man, quit playing games with me, Suki."

"Who said I was playing?" Suki questioned, turning toward him with a raised brow.

"You been gone for a week now. I let you be mad at me because I know I fucked up forgetting our anniversary, but I ain't about to take too much more of this fuck ass attitude you got going on," Jinx grumbled. "It's not even that big of a deal."

"It's not that big of a deal?" Suki asked.

"If you would've brought your ass right back home, you would have known I spent the next day buying you everything to make up for it."

"If I would've brought my ass home?" Suki repeated. "Since we're on the topic of who wasn't home, where were you? Why weren't you home?" Her eyes narrowed into slits as she watched him.

Jinx rubbed the back of his neck, knowing he couldn't answer her question truthfully. Suki may not have been home when he made it in the next morning, but the fact he hadn't been home when she left was bad enough of an insult.

"Out," Jinx answered lamely, not knowing what else to say.

"Out?"

"Yes, Suki. Out," he growled. "I got your point. I fucked up. You gave me a taste of my own medicine by not coming home. Now you back and we can get past this shit."

"Trust, I'm not back by choice," Suki mumbled, giving him her back again.

"What the fuck is that supposed to mean?" Jinx questioned.

"Nothing Jinx," Suki answered louder.

"Nah, you was bold enough to say that shit once, say that shit again," he challenged, stepping further into the room.

"Fine."

Turning to where he now stood, Suki looked at him with a deep-rooted scowl on her face.

"If you hadn't cut off all my cards, I wouldn't be here right now. You could've let me come home when I was ready, but no. Like everything else in this world, it has to be done on Jinx's time," she sassed.

"You damn right! I have the right to cut you off from anything I want to! All this shit belong to me anyways! It's not like you got shit in the first place!"

"AND WHOSE FAULT IS THAT!" Suki snapped.

Jinx's words stung as if he had slapped her in the face. He stood above her, glaring down at her. Jinx knew all about Suki's ambitions in life and like everything else, he took those away from her. He knew if she had too much freedom, she'd leave him the first chance she got, and he had been right. Suki didn't even know the half of Jinx's transgressions and she had bolted at the first sign of fire. She didn't know about his second life and if she did, she'd leave without coming back. Having her completely dependent on him was the only way he could control the situation.

Little did he know, Suki was no longer blind to his bullshit.

"Look Suk," Jinx started, backing away from her and rubbing his eyes. "It was wrong for me to take you off the accounts. I'll go first thing tomorrow morning and put you back on them. But you being home with me is where you're supposed to be."

"Put me back on until when, Jinx? The next time we have a problem and I decide to leave you?" Suki questioned.

Jinx offered her a shrug before he met her eyes again. "Every time you leave, you'll come back. You need me just as much as I need you."

The chilling tone of his voice caused a shiver to run up her spine.

"Until death do us part baby, or did you forget that part?" Jinx asked. Lifting his hand, he used his thumb to wipe away the lonely tear racing down her cheek.

"Awww, don't cry, baby. I'll let you have your space, for now. I'll even have Brick bring some of your clothes before the night is over, but understand that you're mine. I love you too much to let you leave me for good, Suk."

Leaning toward her, Jinx pressed his lips against hers and she felt as if it was the kiss of death. Without offering her any more words, Jinx left her in the room. Air immediately filled her lungs and Suki released a breath she didn't even know she had been holding.

Suki had never heard Jinx talk that way, and the look in his eyes scared her more than she cared to admit. Suki sat down on the bed and buried her face in her hands, attempting to stop the sob that wanted to escape from her lips. The only thing on Suki's mind was who had she married.

———

It had already been a week since Suki had come home and she could feel the depression sinking in. A place she once considered to be her safe haven had slowly started to feel like her prison. Jinx had kept his word and allowed her to stay in the guest bedroom and had even returned her phone and placed her name back on his accounts. Suki had been trying to shake her feelings and get back to being the wife she had always been, but she couldn't. Suki was trapped and the reality was sucking the life out of her.

Scrolling through her phone, Suki pieced together home decor ideas on her Pinterest, trying to give her life some type of normalcy feeling when a tap on her room door caused her to pause her movements.

"Come in," she called out.

"Hello, Señora Bacalao. I was wondering if you needed anything before I left for the evening," their housekeeper, Rosa, questioned with a smile on her face.

Rosa had been a housekeeper at the Bacalao estate since before Suki arrived. Back then she worked seven days a week and stayed in the guest house in the back, but Suki had changed it to three days, telling her she wanted to be able to take care of her husband instead of someone else doing it. Rosa was always nice to Suki, and she appreciated the woman's help whenever she was around.

"No, Rosa, I'm fine," Suki replied, sitting up in the bed and giving the older lady her undivided attention. "And I keep telling you to call me Suki. Mrs. Bacalao makes me sound so old." Suki smirked, causing the older woman to smile in her direction.

"I will try, Señora Suki," Rosa replied in her heavy accent. "Is this how you're going to spend your Friday night?"

"What do you mean?"

"May I say something?"

"Sure." Suki shrugged.

"You seem very sad," Rosa told her. "I normally see you walking around with a smile on your face but lately, I barely see you come out this room and you've even been taking your meals in here."

Suki's small smile instantly vanished as her face fell.

Hearing Rosa refer to her as sad immediately caused Suki's mind to drift to Cheeko. She hadn't texted him since she got her phone back and she felt it would be best to leave the situation alone completely. Suki came with baggage she was sure Cheeko didn't need.

"I say too much," Rosa spoke quickly. "I did not mean to offend you señora."

"You didn't offend me, Rosa. You don't have to apologize," Suki told her. "I guess I just didn't notice my emotions were so obvious."

"Maybe if you got out of the house for a few hours it would make you feel better," Rosa suggested. "Maybe go get some fresh air. You're too young to be stuck indoors all the time. You need to get out and have some fun. It is okay to live your life outside of Señor Bacalao. That is not a crime."

"It's easier said than done. Going outside is boring when you do it alone."

"Then don't do it alone," Rosa told her as if the answer was simple.

Silence fell between the two women as Suki thought about what Rosa said.

"I must get going. My son is visiting tomorrow, and I have not seen him since he moved to New York."

"Goodnight, Rosa, and kiss your grandbaby for me. Don't forget to take lots of pictures for me to see Monday," Suki told her with a smile.

"Of course, señora. Have a good night and think about what I said," Rosa spoke while bowing her head slightly in Suki's direction before turning to leave.

Suki sat in the middle of the queen-sized bed for another ten minutes before easing out of it and leaving the room. Her feet sank into the carpet as she made her way toward the room she shared with Jinx. Opting out of knocking, Suki pushed open the door at the same time Jinx was walking in the room with a towel wrapped around his waist.

Suki allowed her eyes to room over Jinx's body. At 34, his body looked as if he stayed in the gym with his toned arms and six pack. There wasn't a blemish in place. His body was voice of scars or tattoos. Jinx always referred to his body as a temple. He didn't smoke and he barely had more than a glass of liquor at a time. Seeing him in all his glory, Suki could appreciate the way he took care of himself.

"See something you like?" Jinx questioned, catching Suki staring.

Bringing her eyes back to his face, Suki closed the door behind her but didn't move in his direction, instead choosing the lean her back against the wall close to the door.

"I came to tell you I'm going out to get drinks tonight," Suki told him.

"By yourself?"

The last Jinx checked, Suki didn't have any friends and he wasn't fond of the idea of her leaving again so soon after her disappearing act a couple weeks ago.

"No. With a new client of mine," she informed him.

"Client?"

"Yes. While I was gone, I met a client at the lounge around the corner from where I was staying. She had a meeting with one of the employees of the real estate company that left a bad impression on her. So I took it upon myself to fix the situation," Suki told him with a shrug. "She invited me out for drinks afterward to celebrate and I just hadn't gotten back to her about it."

Hearing that she had closed on a property caused Jinx to nod. He knew Suki was very business savvy, but to know she had saved his business money on a whim, Jinx was impressed.

"Okay, but I'd like it if Clarence drove you," Jinx

commented. "Especially since you're going out for drinks," he added.

Suki knew he wanted to keep tabs on her but instead of arguing, she simply agreed.

"Okay."

Suki allowed her eyes to roam the space of their bedroom that seemed to be twice the size of the room she was occupying now. For years this had been her space and now she felt like a stranger in it. Everything was still neat as she left it but any trace of her was absent. Not the light smell of her perfume lingering in the air or the after effects of the candles she loved to burn. The only smells prominent were that of Jinx and his daily routines. Even now.

"Anything else?" Jinx questioned, causing Suki to look back over in his direction.

"I'm going back to work Monday morning," she stated plainly. "Closing the deal, I realized how much I missed working hands on and it'll give me something to do rather than sit home all day and wait for you to grace me with your presence."

She knew the last comment was a low blow, but oh well. Suki had been compromising with Jinx her whole marriage and it was about time she did something she wanted to do for a change, and at the moment, working was that something.

"I can agree to that. Now, can you agree to something for me?"

"Which is?" Suki asked with a raised eyebrow.

"After tonight, you move back into our room. I miss having you in here when I go to sleep and next to me when I wake up in the morning," Jinx admitted. "Even if I do wake up with your hair in my mouth most days," he told her with a slight chuckle.

Suki wanted to protest immediately but instead bit back her words.

"Deal."

"Really?"

Jinx's eyes stretched in surprise, causing Suki to only shrug.

"Marriage only works if you compromise, right?"

"Right," he agreed with a smile.

If sleeping in the bed next to her husband every night was the price Suki had to pay for a little bit of freedom, she was willing to. Rosa made a point, Suki was too young to be stuck in the house all the time with no life of her own outside of Jinx. From this day forward, Suki was determined to live her best life regardless of the hold Jinx felt he had on her.

CHAPTER SEVEN

The atmosphere inside of Treasure's was chill. YG's voice as he rapped his hit "Jealous" sounded over the club as females and dudes rapped along with the lyrics. Cheeko wasn't big on the club scene but after his gun transaction had cleared, Cheeko didn't see a reason not to take the night off. He may have paid two million on the guns he bought from the nigga Jinx, but he had made a five-million-dollar profit on the backend so he wasn't even tripping.

Cheeko's eyes scanned the dance floor from the section he and Nahz had with a few of their workers. His mind was heavy on business as usual. Cheeko had never been the type to get involved in drugs, but when one of his clients offered him ten million to transport his drugs from overseas, Cheeko didn't see why not. There was always a risk in every job Cheeko took but with great risk, there was great reward.

"Damn man, you gon' hog the blunt or you gon' pass that shit," one of their homeboy's named Tone questioned.

Cheeko's eyes followed his gaze to see him staring at Nahz.

"Nigga, fuck nah. This my shit. You want to smoke you better roll yo' own," Nahz shot back.

"Man, that's dirty," Tone replied with a shake of his head.

"So is your shit nigga, but you don't see me complaining."

All Cheeko could do was shake his head as everyone in the section started cracking up at Tone. Nahz had been in a foul mood for the past few days and Cheeko had chosen not to speak on it, thinking whatever it was would pass, but as he watched Nahz bring the bottle of Don Julio to his lips, he knew that he was wrong.

"You better slow down because I ain't carrying your big ass out of here tonight," Cheeko spoke up, getting Nahz's attention.

"You ain't got to because I'm sure before the end of the night I'll have one of these females taking me to her house to take care of a nigga."

"Alright, whatever you say nigga. Just don't get your dumb ass robbed," Cheeko told him, causing Nahz to wave him off.

All Cheeko could do was shake his head before allowing his eyes to go back toward the dance floor. Leaning up, Cheeko thought he saw a familiar face in the crowd before he finally stood to his full height and walked closer to the railing. Watching for a few more seconds, Simone's face turned fully in his direction as she turned around to talk to the person behind her with a smile on her face.

Any other time, Cheeko would have sat back and allowed Simone to do her thing. Everyone knew who she was affiliated with so he never had to worry about her getting in trouble, but her safety wasn't the reason Cheeko couldn't pull his eyes away from where she stood. It was the person she was standing next to who had captured his attention. Cheeko hadn't laid eyes on Suki since the morning he left her hotel room, and to see her in the same building not even 100 feet away had his heart thumping in his chest. It seemed as all the noise in the club had gone silent as his eyes zeroed in on her. The smile she returned to Simone had Cheeko a little jealous. When she hadn't called or sent him a text after he left his number, Cheeko tried to tell himself he understood why she didn't. Suki was a married woman and even if her husband was a clown, he tried to convince himself he couldn't be mad she had went on about her life. But now that she was in his eyesight, all of his understanding went out the window.

"Damn, who is that with Simone?" someone questioned beside him, but he didn't even look to see who it was because whoever had asked, it was irrelevant. Suki wasn't up for grabs to anyone other than him.

"That's what I'm about to go find out," Cheeko said, never taking his eyes from where they stood. He saw them post up at the bar and decided it was time to make his move before they got lost in the crowd.

"Yo, Nahz. Come take this walk with me," Cheeko called out.

Not needing any more information, Nahz took another swig of his bottle before placing it on the table in front of him and standing to his feet. Cheeko walked out of the second floor and took the stairs down. He didn't have to move people out of his way through the crowd. It seemed as if the people parted on their own after seeing him with Nahz trailing behind him. Cheeko had tunnel vision and he couldn't focus on anything else until he made it to his destination.

"Girl, did you see that one nigga hawking you down? He was all in your face," Cheeko could hear Simone laugh as he approached.

"Girl, please. No one was stunting him! Did you see he was missing a front tooth?"

"Hell no. How was I supposed to see that?"

"Hell, I don't know, but I wish like hell I hadn't," Suki joked back, taking a sip of her drink.

As if she could feel his presence, Suki's back straightened up before she began to slowly turn in his direction. The moment her eyes landed on his, she seemed to swallow whatever words she was about to speak next to Simone.

Cheeko's eyes left hers for a moment as he allowed himself to take in her full body. The velvet teal dress she had on clung to her body like a glove and stopped just before it reached the middle of her thigh. He knew that if she bent over, her ass would be on display for the world to see. Her shoulder-length hair was pulled out of her face with a diamond clip that matched the iced-out Cuban link necklace on her neck. She wore a matching Cuban link bracelet and an iced- out AP on her wrist. Everything she had on probably cost more than fifty women's outfits in here combined, but she rocked it well. Cheeko allowed his eyes to meet her face again, only to notice she was checking him out as well.

Cheeko had chosen to rock all black. His entire outfit was Givenchy, minus the Balenciaga sneakers on his feet. He also sported a Cuban link necklace and iced-out Rolex. The pinky ring he wore just set off the rest of his outfit. This wasn't Cheeko the businessman. This was Cheeko the hood nigga out in full effect.

When Suki was done eye fucking him, she brought her eyes back up to meet his before he stepped into her personal space.

"I guess my conversation wasn't good enough for a phone call, huh?" Cheeko questioned in her ear.

The way his smooth baritone and cool breath tickled Suki's ear, she had to press her thighs together to stop the instant thumping of her clit.

"That's not it," Suki told him. "I'm sorry. I just had a chaotic week."

"Too chaotic for you to send me a text? Damn, my feelings a little hurt," Cheeko said, holding his chest.

"That wasn't my intention," Suki told him, speaking loud enough for him to hear her over the music.

"Then make it up to me," he told her before pulling back and looking in her eyes.

Cheeko had purposely not moved too far away, leaving his face only a few inches from hers. If he leaned his head closer, their lips would touch and the way hers were shining under this light, Cheeko wouldn't have minded it at all. They looked soft.

"Well, hello to you too, brother!" Simone shouted, breaking up the staring contest between him and Suki.

"I'm sorry, sis," Cheeko told her, breaking eye contact with Suki.

Stepping out of her space, he moved to the side and gave Simone a hug.

"Come up to the section with us," Cheeko told Simone. "You know this standing and yelling shit not even my style."

"As long as I can pop bottles and dance on the couches, I don't care," Simone told him.

All Cheeko could do was shake his head because he knew she wasn't joking in the slightest. Simone was the life of the party any time they stepped out together and just because she was among new company, Cheeko knew that wouldn't change her demeanor.

"Yeah, I got you sis. Come on," he told her before turning his attention back to Suki. "Let's go," he said, extending his hand out to her.

Without hesitation, Suki placed her hand in Cheeko's and allowed him to ease her off the barstool without allowing her to fall. She wasn't sure why she was so willing to follow this man she barely knew, but she did so without second guessing.

Cheeko held onto Suki's hand the entire time they walked, guiding her through the crowd, never looking back because he knew Nahz had secured Simone for him. Cheeko didn't let go of her hand until they were standing directly in front of the bouncer who moved the rope for them and allowed them inside.

Suki looked back in time to see Simone snatching her hand away from the guy who was helping her through the crowd and push past him inside of the section. His hand found the top of his waves as he mugged her but quickly shook his head before finding a seat and flopping back down.

"You can hang with my sister but before the night's over, I want a little bit of your time," Cheeko's voice said into her ear.

Suki wasn't sure why he had leaned over to speak when it was much quieter up here than the main floor, but she wasn't going to complain. When she invited Simone out tonight, the last person she expected to run into was Cheeko. Simone seemed as shocked as her to see him, so she knew she hadn't been set up.

"Okay," she told him before he gave her a nod and sat next to his friend on the couch. Simone had found an empty couch in the section right across from where Cheeko and the guy sat and had already kicked her shoes off and picked up one of the unopened bottles of Ace of Spades.

Sitting down on the couch next to her, Suki turned her body toward Simone so she wouldn't be tempted to stare at Cheeko all night even though she could feel his eyes on her.

"I don't know what you did to my brother, but you got his nose wide open," Simone commented, pouring the liquor into two glasses on the table.

"I don't know what you're talking about," Suki told her with a wave of her hand.

"Sure, you don't," Simone spoke. "Let's make a toast."

"What are we toasting to?" Suki questioned.

"To newfound friendships and budding love."

"You must be referring to you and the handsome guy who was mugging you, because in case you forgot, I'm married," Suki pointed out, wiggling her ring finger for emphasis.

"Oh, I didn't forget. The question is, did you?" Simone asked, with a knowing look while handing her the cup and clinking it with hers before taking the contents to the head.

Following suit, Suki did the same before she allowed her eyes to turn to where Cheeko sat. His eyes bore into hers as he brought a cup to his lips. Suki couldn't read his expression in the dimly lit area but the way the goosebumps formed on her arms, she could guess what the look meant. Quickly turning her head, Suki tried to focus on the reason she came out tonight. She wasn't trying to get into anything but a little bit of fun. But who's to say Cheeko couldn't be the fun she needed?

For two hours Cheeko watched Suki and Simone dance and take countless drinks to the head. He wasn't trying to interrupt her fun, but being so close to her and not touching her was beginning to drive him insane. Cheeko's eyes watched the curve of her hips as she bent over in front of Simone, causing her ass cheeks to bounce to the beat of some City Girl song. The music seemed to boost their already lit energy, and when he saw the bottom of her ass threatening to spill from her dress as she twerked, he knew he needed to step in. Simone was standing on the couch hyping her up, and Cheeko knew it was almost time to cut her off. She was a grown woman but he was still her older brother and would protect her at any cost.

Suki smelled him before her mind registered him standing over her. His eyes bore down into hers as she stood from her bent over position and stared up at him. His face was expressionless but his eyes told a different story. Suki wasn't sure if he wanted to snatch her up or fuck her right there in the middle of the section for everyone to see. With the way the liquor had Suki feeling, both thoughts excited her to no end.

"Come sit with me for a little bit," Cheeko spoke.

"Don't come over here being a party pooper, Cheek," Simone whined with a slight slur.

Simone was still standing on the couch and was bringing the champagne bottle to her lips. She had abandoned taking shots long ago and had opted to keep the bottle clutched in her fist.

"You need to sit down and sober up some too," Cheeko told her before looking over his shoulder to where Nahz was still sitting.

Nodding his head in Simone's direction, Cheeko watched as Nahz rolled his eyes before standing to his full height.

"Aight, let's go," Nahz said, stepping in front of the section, looking up at Simone.

"Sir, you are not my daddy," Simone hiccuped, pointing a finger at him.

Running his hands down his waves, he gave Simone a look before taking the bottle out of her hand.

"You gone walk or do I gotta carry you out this bitch?" he questioned.

"I'm not going anywhere with you," she told him, hiccuping again. "I'm having fun with my friend."

Nahz turned around to face Cheeko with a raised eyebrow. Only thing Cheeko could do was nod his head. Getting the okay, Nahz pulled Simone from the couch and threw her over his shoulder. Cheeko knew later on when Simone sobered up she'd be pissed at the both of them, but Cheeko didn't need to be trying to keep an eye on Simone while he talked to Suki. Simone and Nahz fought like Tom and Jerry most days, they had since they were kids, but there was no one in this world Cheeko trusted more to protect Simone in his absence.

"Put me the fuck down, Nahz!" Simone yelled, flailing her legs and beating Nahz across the back.

Suki watched in awe as the man she now knew as Nahz turned around to face her and Cheeko, unfazed by Simone's theatrics. Suki could tell he was under the influence as well, but he had sobered up quickly when tasked with taking care of Simone at Cheeko's request.

"You gon' be good?" Nahz asked Cheeko, while Simone wiggled in his grasp.

"Yeah, I'ma chill for a little bit more before heading out," Cheeko informed him. "Just let me know when you get her home safe."

"Bet," Nahz replied before looking down at Suki and offering her a head nod.

Cheeko watched Nahz grab Simone's belongings in one hand without losing his grip on her before leaving the section. Seeing Nahz depart, the few members left of his team gave him a head nod and followed Nahz out, leaving Suki and Cheeko alone in the section.

Grabbing a hold of her hand, Cheeko guided Suki back to where he was originally sitting before pulling her down on the couch beside him. He wasn't trying to overstep by placing her on his lap, but he wanted her as close to him as possible.

Suki's eyes closed momentarily as her feet screamed. She had been up dancing on her feet all night and her feet were definitely starting to feel it. She wasn't the least bit upset though, because for the fun she had been having, enduring a little pain was worth it.

"You good?" Cheeko's question invaded her thoughts, causing her to open her eyes and look over at him.

"Yeah. Feet just throbbing a little," she admitted.

"Let me see."

"Excuse me?" she asked, his request throwing her off slightly.

"Your feet," Cheeko clarified. "Put them in my lap. Let me see."

Suki hesitated for a moment before easing away from him some and bringing her feet up onto his lap. Suki watched with curiosity as he began to unbuckle her heel with care before pulling it off and doing the same with the other. Relief instantly washed over Suki's body at the release of pressure her shoes were causing.

"Cute," Cheeko commented.

Suki went to ask him what he meant, but the feeling of him wrapping his hand around her foot and kneading away the kinks caused all thoughts to escape her brain momentarily. Her eyes lowered and her head fell back against the arm of the couch as his hands moved along her foot, giving her a foot massage she didn't even know she needed.

Cheeko watched the look of euphoria on her face as he gave her the massage, and his mind went to the gutter for a split second. He wondered if the same look of ecstasy would cross her face as his dick invaded her walls and caused her to leak her essence all over him. The feeling of his dick twitching instantly brought him back to the present where his eyes drifted to where her hands rested across her lap.

The glittering of her diamond ring under the dim light was a reminder she was off limits to him. And even if he knew being with her was forbidden, he couldn't help wanting to be in her presence.

Comfortable silence remained between them as Cheeko massaged each of Suki's feet. Opening her eyes, she looked at him with hooded vision. The liquor in her system along with the way he was touching her ever so softly, caused Suki's center to clench. Her eyes followed to his lap as she watched his hands moved over her foot with precision. His hands engulfed her small feet and were soft to the touch, even though they held a certain roughness to them. The callouses letting Suki know he wasn't afraid to work with his hands. His thumb digging into the center of her foot caused a moan to escape Suki.

Hearing the sound pass through her lips, Cheeko's hands instantly stilled. Meeting her gaze, the look of bliss hadn't left her face, but there was something more dancing behind her eyes.

"Stop looking at me like that," Cheeko warned in a low voice.

"Like what?"

"If you don't know, I won't tell you, but if you keep on doing it, I can't be held accountable for my actions."

Instead of backing down the way Cheeko thought she would, Suki continued to stare at him. Seeing how far she was willing to go, Cheeko allowed one of his hands to move from her foot and begin inching up her leg. Suki followed the movement with her eyes, her breathing becoming heavier the further his hand went. When he reached her thigh, his hand stopped moving, causing Suki to stare at him. Cheeko saw no resistance in her eyes and allowed his hand to move again until his fingers began to move upward across her thigh. Unconsciously, Suki's thighs parted ever so slightly, inviting Cheeko's hand to travel there.

"Look at me," Cheeko coaxed.

Following the command, Suki gave Cheeko her eyes as his hand continued. Tingles raced up Suki's thighs at his touch and even though she knew she should stop him, she couldn't. The way her body reacted to him had Suki wanting to allow her legs to fall open completely and he hadn't done anything but caress her thigh.

"Come."

The word didn't come out as a question but more of a demand. Cheeko leaned back to his original spot, taking his hand with him as he pulled away from her. Suki's skin immediately missed the texture and warmth of his hand. Not needing any time to think about his order, Suki leaned up and prepared to straddle his waist in the tight dress she wore.

"Ahnt, ahnt." Cheeko stopped her. "The other way," he instructed.

Easing off the couch, Suki stood to her feet and watched Cheeko position himself, so he was comfortable before signaling with his finger for her to turn around. Turning her body, Suki gave Cheeko her back. She felt his hands grip each side of her hips before pulling her into his lap. Using his knee, Cheeko nudged Suki's legs apart so she would sit on him with her legs open slightly. Placing one hand on her thigh, Cheeko used the other to snake up the front of Suki's body until his hand was placed gently around her neck. Guiding her body back to his, Cheeko rested Suki's back against his chest but didn't move his hand.

Suki's heart beat wildly in her chest as Cheeko applied light pressure to the side of her neck. His lips found her ear and the feel of his warm tongue against the sensitive skin caused Suki's breath to catch in her throat. As if instinctively, Suki went to close her legs to ease the throb, but Cheeko's hand prevented her from doing so.

"Do you want to stop?" Cheeko inquired, his voice low and thick with desire.

"No," Suki replied, the gruffness of her own voice sounding foreign to her ears.

Cheeko allowed the hand on her thigh to ease its way up until he could feel the heat from her center against his hand. He had to close his eyes for a second because he almost said fuck all the foreplay, but he had to remind himself this wasn't about what he wanted. Pushing up the fabric of her dress some, Cheeko allowed his fingers to move along the lace material of her panties, instantly feeling how drenched they were. His fingers stroked slowly up the center, where he knew her lips divided. The meatiness of her lips caused Cheeko's finger to sink slightly before he felt Suki's swollen nub underneath the material.

Cheeko applied light pressure, causing Suki to inhale sharply. As if they had a mind of their own, Suki's hips began to rock against Cheeko's hand, wanting him to apply more pressure. Nothing about what she was allowing Cheeko to do was right, but the ache she felt was the only thing currently on her mind. Suki would worry about the consequences or guilt of her actions later but at the moment, she didn't feel any.

Cheeko pulled his hand away, leaving a sudden yearning for him to place it back where it was.

"Tell me what you need, Suki," Cheeko spoke directly into her ear. "I won't guess, and I won't assume. You have to tell me what you want."

"I want," Suki nearly panted, "I want you to touch me."

"Through your panties?" Cheeko asked.

Shaking her head from side to side, Suki didn't want a barrier between them. She wanted to feel the soft yet callous texture that had soothed her feet against the sensitive flesh of her swollen yoni.

"Use your words," Cheeko instructed, gently squeezing the side of her neck.

Even though he was barely touching her, Cheeko could feel as more wetness came leaking from between her lower lips. Tilting her head to the side, Cheeko ran his tongue against the side of her neck before nibbling the same spot. Everything about his current situation was out of the norm for him. Not only was he looking to pleasure a woman who belonged to someone else, but he was doing it in a public place. The seclusion of the VIP section and the dim lights kept anyone from seeing what they were doing, but the carelessness of it all had Cheeko's dick stiffening in his jeans. All it took was one person to walk by and they would be busted. Cheeko knew all of that and still he didn't want to stop.

"No," Suki finally called out.

"No, what?"

"I don't want you to touch me through my panties. I want you to touch me for real."

At her admittance, Cheeko removed his hand from around her throat and placed it close to his other hand. He parted her legs over his thighs, giving him more access to her center. Suki felt each of his hands on the top of her panties and her heart beat with anticipation.

"Can I tear these off?" Cheeko's question caused another thump to greet her clit as she realized he didn't want to waste time easing her out of her panties or simply moving them to the side. He wanted her completely exposed for him to follow through with what she wanted.

"Yes," Suki replied breathily.

Getting a good grip on either sides of the material, Cheeko tugged, and the ripping sound was music to his ears. Suki's body shuddered lightly as a breeze passed over her sudden exposed wetness. As if Cheeko could read her thoughts, he placed his hand back in its original spot on her neck and squeezed, causing the urge to close her legs to subside.

"Don't."

Suki simply nodded as his other hand found her slippery folds. Her eyes closed as his finger brushed against her swollen clit before his pinched it between two of his fingers. The act almost made Suki cream instantly. Amused by her reaction,

Cheeko continued to tug on her clit as a moan rose in her throat. He could tell she was trying to keep her voice down, but Cheeko wanted to hear her, even if it was only for his ears.

"Move your body so your face is in my neck but don't close your legs," Cheeko instructed, never stopping the circular movements and tugs he was delivering but moving his other arm so she could adjust in his lap.

Suki didn't protest, just move comfortably so she could do as he asked. Once her face was buried in his neck, her hand instinctively found its way to his head where her fingers intertwined with his dreads.

"If you need to moan, do it against my neck but don't hold it back. You understand?"

Suki nodded her headed into his neck, causing Cheeko to pinch her clit hard.

"I didn't hear you," he told her.

"Yes," she moaned, gripping his dreads in her hand.

"Good girl."

Not wanting to waste any more time. Cheeko slid his fingers down the folds through her stickiness until his fingers were lined with her opening. Easing two fingers inside of her, Suki's walls instantly sucked him in, and a moan escaped her lips. Using his other hand, Cheeko started to rub in circular motions against her clit as his fingers eased in and out of her. Same as before, Suki began to move her hips so that she was rocking onto his fingers as if she were riding his dick. Instead of stopping like before, Cheeko continued his assault into her wetness, picking up the pace as more of her juices eased out onto his fingers and dripped down his hand.

Cheeko knew without a doubt the front of his pants were as good as ruined, but the feel of Suki's insides and the sound of her moans against his skin had him saying to hell with them. With the skills of an experienced lover, Cheeko worked

Suki's insides until the feeling of her pending release started to build up inside of her. Her walls began to clench harder around Cheeko's fingers, causing him to move the angle until he was stroking upward, tickling the tip of her G-spot.

"Fuckkkk, Cheekoooo," Suki's voice called out. It was muffled but he heard her loud and clear.

The sound of his name falling from her lips in ecstasy was enough for Cheeko to pick up his pace. Sliding the tip of a finger directly under her bud, Cheeko pushed his other fingers deeper inside her.

"Nut for me, Suki," he commanded in a low voice, causing Suki's body to momentarily go stiff before liquid started rushing out of her.

"Ahhhhhhhhh," Suki moaned loudly, gripping his dreads tightly and pressing her face into his neck where he felt her teeth graze his skin.

Cheeko didn't stop moving his fingers but started working them faster inside of her, causing her juices to splash out against his hands and make a wet sound as they sprayed out across her. Cheeko would have never guessed Suki was a squirter, but his eyes locked on her release as she began to go limp in his arms. His fingers worked her completely through her orgasm until it began to subside. Suki's chest rose and fell hard against Cheeko as she tried to catch her breath. Suki had never nutted so hard in her life and even though she wanted to blame it on the alcohol, she couldn't because she had been drunk plenty of times and received a dick down from Jinx, but none of them ever resulted in her squirting so hard to the point she lost all her senses.

Cheeko didn't say anything to Suki as he eased his wet hands out of her. She lifted her head in time to see Cheeko bringing them to his lips and sucking on them with a groan. His eyes found hers, but he never stopped what he was doing.

He licked each of his fingers clean while staring deep in her eyes.

"Now what?" Suki asked, through bated breath.

"Now," Cheeko started. "I send you home..." His voice trailed off slightly before he spoke his next words with disdain, "To your man."

The thought of going home to Jinx caused an aching feeling in her chest, but Suki nodded her head slowly as if she understood. Temporary pleasure couldn't change the fact she was a married woman. As Suki stood to her feet and watched as Cheeko used napkins and the melted ice to help her clean herself up as best he could, she knew nothing was going to keep her from seeing him again. She had fought the urge to be in his presence for over a week now and Suki didn't want to fight it anymore. She didn't know what she expected to come from her interactions with Cheeko. All Suki knew for sure was, being in Cheeko's presence was the safest Suki had felt in her whole life. Not even Jinx brought her the peace Cheeko did and even if it was wrong, Suki was determined to find a way to make it right.

CHAPTER EIGHT

Nahz brought the blunt to his lips as he watched the subtle rise and fall of Simone's chest. She was passed out in his passenger seat as they sat outside her house, but Nahz couldn't bring himself to wake her up. Being away from her since their fight was torturing him in the worst way, but his pride wouldn't allow him to call her. All he could do was submerge himself into work to keep his mind off her, but it wasn't helping.

Seeing her tonight caused his heart to still in his chest and all Nahz wanted to do was tell her they could go back to the way things were if he could just sit in her presence, but he knew that's not what he wanted. Nahz was a fucked-up nigga, had always been since his younger days terrorizing the streets, so he wasn't sure if having someone like Simone was what he deserved. But damn did he want her.

6lack's voice was the only thing giving him background noise to his thoughts. It was well after two in the morning and Simone's neighborhood was void of any life; that didn't stop Nahz's constant surveillance of their surroundings though.

Nahz had been biting back his anger all night watching Simone dance on couches and shake her ass with her homegirl not even ten feet from where he sat. Usually, Nahz didn't mind letting her enjoy herself and having fun because he knew she would be in his bed at the end of it all but tonight, things had been different. He had to watch at a distance while she got outside of her body, rapping songs about being a get money ass bitch who didn't need a nigga.

Nahz knew her words were directed at him even though he had done nothing wrong in his eyes. Was it wrong he wanted to love her out in the open regardless of the drama it caused him? Was it wrong he was a grown ass man who was tired of hiding? He had been sleeping with Simone for two years and what had started out as just a fuck thing, blossomed into so much more.

In the beginning, Nahz still ran the streets and knocked different bitches down, but then one day something changed. Without even noticing the change, he only started making time for her. He no longer wanted to be in the streets chasing but have her waiting on him in one of his t-shirts while she cooked one of his favorite meals, waiting on him so binge watch some sappy Netflix show with her.

Before Nahz knew it, Simone had domesticated him without even trying and he would never disrespect her by sleeping with someone else. But every time Nahz wanted to come clean to Cheeko about their relationship, Simone found a way to talk him out of it. Nahz was tired, but he'd be lying if he said he didn't miss her.

The sound of groaning coming from beside him pulled Nahz from his thoughts as he watched Simone stir in her sleep. Her eyes fluttered open slowly as she looked around trying to remember where she was. Her head throbbed slightly and her mouth felt like sandpaper.

"Drink this," Nahz told her, offering her a bottle of water.

Without hesitation, Simone adjusted her body in the seat before accepting it. Simone was glad for the soft butter leather seats of Nahz's Benz truck. She was sure if she were sleeping anywhere else in the position she was in, she'd have a crook in her neck.

"Thank you," Simone mumbled before opening the bottle and bringing it to her lips.

The cool liquid soothed her dry throat immediately. She took another swig before closing it, prepared to hand it back to Nahz.

"Keep it," he declined.

Simone watched out the corner of her eye as Nahz brought his blunt back to his lips but made no attempt to adjust in his seat as if he were ready for her to leave. After the way they had left things, Simone thought he would be ready to get rid of her but no; he was laid back and relaxed as ever as he sat reclined in his seat.

The Sauvage cologne Nahz loved was caressing her nostrils and she just wanted to climb inside his skin and stay there. Simone may have acted out on him at the club and talked major shit but now sitting here in his presence, she was as quiet as a church mouse. The tension in the air between them was thick but Simone was in no hurry to leave him. She couldn't remember the last time she had gone more than a week without seeing Nahz, and she realized she missed him more than she cared to admit.

Nahz watched her fidget with her fingers with her eyes casted down in her lap. He could feel the anxiety pouring out of her and a part of him wanted to lean over the armrest and kiss all her apprehension away, but what good would that do? What signals would it be sending if he just gave in every single time just to get back on her good side? Nahz was always the one to compromise. Showing Simone over and over again how much he loved her and would fight for her, but when would she show him?

"So, what we doing, Simone?" Nahz inquired, tired of beating around the bush.

"You tell me," Simone countered. "You're the one who kicked me out of your house. Not the other way around."

"It was either ask you to leave or fuck you up for playing in my face. Again."

"When have I ever played in your face, Nahzir?" Simone questioned, turning her body in the seat so she could face him.

Her face was twisted up but Nahz didn't care.

"When don't you play in my face, Simone?" Nahz retorted. "I'm a grown ass man, yet you got me sneaking around as if I'm some little ass boy."

"You didn't used to care about us sneaking around before but now suddenly, it's a problem."

"It was just sex before," Nahz told her.

"It's just sex now!" Simone shot back before her hand flew to her mouth, realizing her mistake.

Nahz's eyes narrowed at her. The only light shining in the car was from his radio and the street light outside, barely illuminating the car, but Simone could still see the deadly shift on Nahz's face as he stared at her. She hadn't meant for those words to fall from her lips, but they had, and the way he was glaring at her, let her know it was too late to take them back.

"What did you say?" The iciness of his tone made Simone's heart pang before her heart started to race.

"Nahz, I—"

"Don't, 'Nahz' me, Simone!" Nahz snapped, cutting her off. "What. Did. You. Say?" he questioned, enunciating ever word.

"I said it was still just sex," Simone mumbled, her eyes falling to her lap again.

Silence fell between them before the sound of a chuckle passed through Nahz's lips. Simone's head snapped in his direction as she watched him laugh from the depths of his soul. Something about him laughing didn't sit right with her and caused uneasiness to settle over her.

"I don't even know why I'm surprised," Nahz started once his laughter began to die down. "No matter how many times I try to do right by you, you turn around and show me a nigga don't mean nothing to you."

Simone didn't know what to say as she watched him lean up in his seat. His hands rested on the steering wheel as he brought his eyes back toward her. His eyes held no emotion as his eyes raked her body before he scoffed and shook his head. Turning his eyes straight ahead, Nahz didn't look at her as he spoke.

"Yo, get out."

"Huh?"

"I said get out," he replied flatly.

"So that's it, you're kicking me out again?" Simone questioned, craning her neck back. "All because what? 'Cause I hurt your feelings? You're being really emotional right now, Nahzir," Simone told him with a roll of her eyes.

"Shit, call it whatever you want, shorty," Nahz responded with a shrug. "Maybe I am being emotional, but I know what I'm not about to continue to be, a toy for you to play with. You want a nigga that's just out to fuck you and is content with sneaking around with you forever? Cool. Go find him, Mone, because it's no longer me. Now with that being said, get out."

When he didn't hear her moving beside him, he turned back in her direction to find her staring at him with a mug on her face.

"Problem?" he asked, his head tilting to the side.

"Fuck you, Nahzir," Simone huffed, picking up her things, reaching for the door handle.

"Nah. I'm good," Nahz told her nonchalantly. "Now hurry up and get inside so I can slide," he spoke before turning away from her.

The Benz vibrated hard from the strength at which Simone slammed the door, signifying her attitude, but Nahz didn't feed into it. Simone was spoiled and she'd act out the moment something didn't go her way. The old Nahz would have ran after her to either reprimand her for what she had done or try to chase away the hurt he saw in her eyes, but he couldn't do it anymore. Time and time again, Simone showed him where he stood in her life, and now it was time he showed her he wouldn't always be waiting when she turned around.

CHAPTER NINE

J inx winced at the tenderness of his dick as he washed his body underneath the stream of water from the shower. Flashes of Suki riding him like a jockey when she got home the night before plagued his mind. She had come in half drunk from the club, taken a shower, and rode him until she finally collapsed beside him. Jinx didn't know what had gotten into her but if giving her a little freedom was all it took to have her riding his dick without question, he was all for it. The only downside was his dick felt completely useless this morning. Jinx washed his body one more time before turning the water off and stepping out of the shower. It was going on twelve in the afternoon and while Suki was still curled in their bed catching Z's, Jinx had moves to make.

It was time for his quarterly sit down with his connect. He told Jinx he had important business to discuss with him and Jinx could practically feel the money touching his fingertips. Jinx had his hand in pretty much anything where money was involved. From drugs to guns, corporate to illegal, he was the man to come see. He had the best product touching the street and his plug had the purest cocaine to touch the West Coast in the past three years. After Jinx finished brushing his teeth at the sink, he walked into the bedroom where he found Suki sitting up in the middle of the bed. She was so busy clicking away on her phone, she hadn't noticed him emerge from the bathroom.

"Good to see you're awake," Jinx called out to her, causing her eyes to snap in his direction with a quick second of surprise on her face.

Jinx's antennae went up, but Suki's face was back to normal in a split second, replacing her shock with a small smile.

"Yeah," Suki started. "I'm surprised I don't have a hang-over," Suki told him, her phone buzzing in her hand.

Jinx watched her for a few seconds as she smiled down at her screen, typing again as if he weren't in the room, before he began walking to his closet. Her mood seemed lighter than it had been since she came back home, and Jinx began to question why but quickly brushed it off, remembering the early morning they had.

Good dick will make a bitch act right, Jinx thought. *Have her singing a different tune.*

Jinx left Suki in the room so he could get dressed for his meeting. Knowing the meeting was business casual, Jinx chose a pair of beige slacks with a black button up and completing the look, he slid his feet into a pair of black Stacy Adams loafers. Jinx looked himself over in the mirror before undoing the top buttons of his shirt and letting it open slightly. Suki always joked that he looked like a younger version of Esai Morales without the salt and pepper hair due to his Hispanic features being so dominant. His mother was black, but Jinx barely took after her because he looked so much like his father. Regardless of his heritage, Jinx knew he looked damn good.

Jinx didn't have to worry about brushing his hair because his barber had gotten him together a few days prior. All he needed to do was spray on some cologne, grab a few pieces of jewelry, and he was set to go. Looking down at his wedding band on his left finger, Jinx glanced over his shoulder to make sure Suki was not coming before he slid it from his finger. Sliding the ring into his jewelry box, Jinx stuffed his left hand in his pocket before walking out to see Suki still in the same spot.

As far as Jinx's connect knew, he was a single man. He had been very careful not to divulge that part of his life. Jinx wanted to appear as a man with no weaknesses and nothing to hold him back. It was the very reason he had never put Suki's name on anything outside of his bank accounts and if she ever decided to leave him, she'd be left with nothing. Thank God for prenups. His connect Hector had hinted plenty of times to have a young daughter he wanted to marry off soon since she was the only heir to his business. He wanted to go back home with his wife and play the background, but he couldn't do so without finding a suitable match for his daughter and as fucked up as it may sound, Jinx wanted to be that match.

Jinx may have had ties to both Suki and Marina, but if it came between them and becoming the plug's son-in-law, there was no comparison. He knew Marina would fall in line because she knew how to play her part. The only wild card in the whole game was Suki, but Jinx had ways of making her behave if it ever came down to that. He just prayed it never did.

"Where you headed?" Suki questioned, with a raised eyebrow, her eyes roaming across his body.

Jinx had let his thoughts lead him somewhere else, so he hadn't even noticed she was looking in his direction.

"I have lunch with a colleague. Thinking about investing in more land for the construction company," Jinx told her.

"But it's Sunday."

"Business is business," was his only response as he shrugged.

Suki's eyes watched him suspiciously before turning away. Jinx watched as she placed her phone on the nightstand and got out of bed.

"That's fine," Suki told him, walking toward the bathroom. "I thought we could do something together, but I'll probably just head to the mall instead."

"Sorry babe," Jinx offered. "This is just very important, but we can do something when we both get home later on."

Suki didn't turn around as he talked, just continued walking, and he could tell she was pissed.

"How about you take my black card? Maybe even invite your new client you went out with last night and make it a girls' day. Y'all can put everything on me," Jinx suggested, walking to the bathroom door and watching as she stripped out of her clothes.

A smile spread across her face at hearing she could spend money without any consequences, and Suki immediately perked up.

"I guess that could work," she told him with a coy smile on her face.

Jinx returned her smile, realizing he got her. He knew Suki wouldn't turn down a free shopping trip and if he was lucky, him suggesting she take her newfound friend with her would get him back in her guts by tonight. If he was really lucky, she might even bless him with her million-dollar mouth. Out of all the bitches he had, no one's head game compared to his wife's. She was just a throat goat as they called it.

"Alright, I gotta head out," Jinx spoke. "But I'll see you when you get home tonight."

Suki waltzed her naked body in his direction before standing on her tip toes and planting a kiss to his lips. Jinx used his right hand to grab a handful of her ass and pulled her closer, sucking on her bottom lip. When she began pulling away, Jinx smacked her on the ass, causing her to yelp slightly with a devilish grin.

"See you later," she told him, backing away headed back toward the shower.

Jinx admired her body momentarily before he shook his head and turned to leave the room.

Yeah, I gotta give her more freedom more often, he thought, leaving her to handle her business.

———

It took Jinx thirty minutes to make it to the location Hector wanted to meet at. He checked his watch and realized he had about five minutes to spare to get inside before Hector chewed him out or worse, canceled the meeting altogether until the next time he wanted to talk. Hector hated when his time was wasted. He saw it as a sign of disrespect but in Jinx's eyes, he never felt it was that deep. Shit came up. Traffic could have you delayed or in his case, he could be trying to con his wife into giving him a replay of the good sex they had. Jinx hated being on another man's time but if he wanted to stay in good graces with the man, he had to suck it up and make some sacrifices until he got what he wanted.

Jinx was let into the house and searched, even though he wasn't dumb enough to bring his gun to a meeting. Hector's people would put a bullet between his eyes before he made it down the hallway. He hadn't even brought Brick with him as protection. Hector was that serious about his privacy and space. Jinx followed behind one of the bodyguards down a long hallway until he was led to a room. Jinx watched as the guard knocked on the door, before he heard Hector's voice come from the other side.

"*Ingresar!*"

Opening the door, the guard stayed in the hallway but moved to the side to allow Jinx inside the room. Jinx was impressed by how Hector had them trained. In the past three years, he had never heard them speak and he barely saw them enter rooms unless instructed to do so by Hector. Jinx couldn't wait until he had the type of pull Hector had.

"Ahh, Jonathan! You made it," Hector greeted, addressing Jinx by his government. "And pushing it with the time as always," Hector commented, not standing from his seat.

Jinx walked over and extended his hand to the man as a sign of respect but didn't offer him an explanation. Hector hated them.

"I'll do better in the future," Jinx replied instead.

"I would hope so," Hector told him. "Please sit. I know you are a busy man," Hector said, gesturing to the chair in front of his desk.

Jinx took a seat and leaned back, waiting to hear what Hector had to say.

"I got the report you sent last week along with the money," Hector started. "Everything was in order as always. I am very pleased."

"Gracias, Hector. Means a lot."

"I called you here not to discuss our usual business, but to let you know there will be new changes happening within the next two months. My wife Ester is on my back about being in the states. She believes it is too dangerous for a man of my caliber to be traveling back and forth so much. So, that means I have to appoint someone to handle my shipments from overseas to stateside and back again."

Jinx tried to keep his expression vacant of any excitement as he listened to Hector. Jinx already knew where this conversation was headed, and he was more than ready to step into Hector's shoes.

"Your wife is a cautious woman. You have to respect that," Jinx commented.

"Si, which is why I'm heeding her words," Hector agreed with a nod. "I'm not as young as I once was, and I am more than ready to kick my feet back and handle things from the comfort of my homeland."

"So, what are you thinking?"

"We have a good working relationship, you and me. You give me no troubles, so I want to keep the relationship going." Hector paused. "With that being said—"

"Hector, I don't know what to say," Jinx spoke, cutting him off. "I've never moved weight on the scale you're asking but I'm sure with your guidance, I can keep things running smoothly."

Hector's eyebrow lifted slightly before recognition lit up on his face as he chuckled lightly and shook his head.

"Oh, you misunderstand, compadre," Hector started. "I am not asking you to take over for me. I was simply telling you that I will still supply your drugs for you, but you will be going through someone else for your pickup and drop-offs," Hector explained. "I already had a man in mind when I made the decision to back away. Well, two actually. It took some convincing on my part to get him to agree to my terms but as you know, money talks."

"Oh."

"Don't be disappointed, Johnathan. Even though drugs is not this young man's particular forte, he has a certain *some-*

thing you can appreciate when it comes to business. He reminds me much of myself. I just wish I had his mind when I was his age," Hector commented with another laugh but a look of admiration and respect on his face. "As long as you continue working the way you are working, I don't see any problems arising. You will still get your drugs from me. Your money will still come to me. The only thing changing is the person you see and the operation. He will be in charge of pickups and drop-offs for shipments but other than that, everything will remain the same."

Jinx didn't talk for a second as he let Hector's words sink in. For three years he had been building for a higher position and in the blink of an eye, it was taken away from him. To learn he wasn't taking a step up but someone was coming in above him was a low blow, and to add insult to injury, whoever this guy was didn't even move weight for a living. To say Jinx was mad would be an understatement; he was livid, but knew better than to show it on his face.

"When is this change supposed to take place?" Jinx questioned.

"I have to iron out the last-minute details but before I make the complete transition, I will hold a meeting for a sit down with all three of you to make introductions. At the time, we will talk changes he feels comfortable making along with whatever concerns you may have. Once the meeting is over, everything the following month will be set to move on those terms. Entendes?"

Jinx just gave a nod, causing a smile to split across Hector's face.

"Good. Good," Hector spoke, clapping his hands together. "The boys have already worked out your shipment to last you until the sit down. Everything should be ready to go when you get outside."

Jinx knew Hector was dismissing him, so he simply nodded his head again before shaking the man's hand and leaving the room. If Jinx was a cartoon character, smoke would visibly be coming from his ears. Jinx would do what Hector asked for the time being, but Jinx had to find a way to get to the top. He didn't care who he had to shit on or step on to get there.

CHAPTER TEN

Marina's foot tapped impatiently as she stared down at her phone. Jinx had ignored yet another one of her text messages and still hadn't returned any of her calls. After he spent an entire week at her house with her and the boys, Marina was sure things between them would soon become official. He hadn't said it out of his mouth to her, but Marina knew his wife had left him the night he didn't come home. She had overheard his conversation with someone questioning if she had made it back and all Marina could do was smile.

Jinx had left her bed one morning the same as he had been doing, telling her he'd be back later that night after he handled business, but he never showed up. She had been calling and texting him nonstop since and he simply fell off the face of the earth. The first night, Marina was worried about him, thinking something bad had happened. She had called every hospital and morgue in the city looking for him. When she came up empty, she finally caved in and tapped into the tracker she had placed on his phone one day. Marina had never seen the need to use it because Jinx was always upfront with her about where he was going and what he was doing. When his location finally popped up, she realized he was home.

Determined to get some answers, Marina drove to the home he owned with his wife, ready to confront him. Only to find his wife at the gate in the back of an Uber. Marina was pissed. She sat in her car and watched her drive into the gate before it closed behind her. Marina knew it was irrational for her to be mad, his wife was pulling up to *their* house, but she was. All she could do was sit in her car and stare with envy. Suki had everything Marina wanted and deserved. She was the one who had his kids. She was the one who had been holding him down for years. Not her. Marina had been the faithful side chick. Sucking and fucking Jinx at his every whim, and what did she get? Nothing, while his bitch of a wife got everything. She didn't even appreciate Jinx.

Marina thought by exposing Jinx's second life, Suki would leave him, and he would come running to her. And he had, but it was only temporary. He gave Marina the life she wanted for a week but the moment his wife came home, he was treating her as if she didn't exist. Marina knew if Jinx learned what she had done, he would have killed her by now, but he hadn't, so it made her wonder what the cause of his newfound attitude was.

Seeing he wasn't going to respond yet again, Marina threw her phone down in frustration. Plopping down hard on her bed, Marina snatched a pillow to scream into. She was annoyed but she didn't want to wake the boys, who she'd just put down for a nap. If Marina was being completely honest with herself, she never wanted to be a mom. She simply wanted a way to keep Jinx around. When he met Suki, Marina could tell instantly she was losing him. He was pulling the same moves he was now. Once she realized she needed to one up Suki, Marina came up with a plan to give him the one thing Suki didn't: a baby.

Jinx may have been a piece of shit as a human being most days, but Marina had to admit he was a damn good father to his boys, and now they were having a daughter. She knew he would dote on his baby girl the same as the other two. Marina's hand subconsciously rubbed her swollen belly, when her baby delivered a sharp kick to her side.

"Calm down, baby girl. Mama's thinking of a way to get your daddy home for good," Marina talked out loud as if the baby could truly understand what she was saying.

As if on cue, the baby kicked again, causing Marina to wince slightly before a wicked grin spread across her face.

Smiling down at her stomach, Marina went to grab the phone she had discarded a moment ago and went to her contact list. Finding the number she was looking for, she pressed the phone icon. Marina eased out of the room and made her way to her living room where she sat on the couch listening to the phone trill. Marina got slightly discouraged thinking the call would be sent to voicemail, until the phone call was connected.

"Hello?"

"Hey bitch." Marina smiled. "You busy?"

"Actually, yeah. I'm at work. Making my rounds headed to see one of my patients."

"That's actually why I was calling," Marina said. "I need a favor."

CHAPTER ELEVEN

Suki's nerves were all over the place as she looked at the address on her phone again and back up to the number on the door. When Suki told Jinx she would spend the day at the mall shopping until she dropped, she had every intention of doing just that. How she had ended up standing on a door step clear across the city, Suki wasn't sure, but she was here now. Suki tried to hide her nervousness as a woman with a dog stepped out into the hall headed toward the elevator. Suki smiled at the woman awkwardly, causing the woman to give her a small unsure smile in return. Suki's mind was playing tricks on her as she imagined a big scarlet A on her chest everyone could see. Suki waited until the woman was out of sight before she brought her hand up and knocked lightly on the door.

The minute Suki stood waiting for the door to be opened felt like a lifetime as paranoia began to seep in. She jumped lightly at the sound of the door being opened as she bounced from foot to foot. Cheeko stared down into her face curiously, wondering what had her so worked up. If he hadn't been walking from the kitchen at the time, he would have never heard the light raps against his door.

"Hi," Suki greeted just above a whisper. She wasn't even sure he had heard her because the look on his face never changed as he moved to the side to allow her access into his home.

Stepping in cautiously, Suki walked a few steps before stopping as he closed and locked the door behind her. She waited patiently until he walked around her and headed deeper into the house. Following him further inside, Suki took in the decor of his house and had to admit she was impressed. His living room reminded her of Tommy Buns's house off *Belly* with the stark-white walls, black couches, and black and white pictures that hung on the wall.

Suki stopped her gawking as she realized he was still walking and picked up her pace to keep up with him. Her eyes fell on his shirtless back and the massive collection of tattoos displayed there. It looked like a mural. Her eyes followed the details and the story it told. Black activists were in full view on his back along with black icons and even tragic stories of our history. Suki wanted to trace the lines of the piece, her eyes falling on the portraits of Malcolm X, Rosa Parks, Bob Marley, and even Emmitt Till.

Cheeko turning to the right caught her attention as he stepped into a room that was set up like a small in-home theater. Suki looked around as Cheeko turned around to give her his attention. Her eyes followed his and she tried hard not to stare. Suki had noticed the gray sweatpants he had on the moment he opened his door but attempted to keep her eyes on his face. She hadn't seen the outline of any briefs or boxers as she followed him, leading her to believe he didn't have any on. The thought of it caused Suki to fidget again.

"If you were nervous about coming over here, shorty, you could've just told me no," Cheeko finally said.

"I'm not nervous about being here," she told him, looking up into his eyes.

Every time Suki was in his presence, she had to stop herself from doing something off impulse. Her eyes fell to his lips for a moment before snapping back up to his eyes. Images of him sucking her juices off his fingers flooded Suki's mind, causing her to break eye contact.

"Then why won't you look at me?"

"It's just hard to concentrate with you being shirtless is all," Suki told him. Suki wanted to kick herself for the childish answer, but it was the only one she could think of to explain why she was so jumpy.

Truth was, Suki was extremely nervous but not for the reasons Cheeko thought. Suki's mind kept going back to their time in the club, and now that he was standing in front of her, she wanted nothing more than to finish what they started. All the while, he looked as if what happened between them didn't faze him at all.

Cheeko's eyes racked over Suki's body, taking in her body language. The smell of her perfume had captured his attention the moment he opened his door and he had to remind himself she wasn't his girl. He allowed his eyes to roam over the curve of her hips in the skinny-strapped, form-fitting sundress she had on. There was a plunging neckline, which gave a nice view of her perky breasts without overdoing it. Without her turning around, he already knew her ass was sitting nice behind her. Her feet were in a pair of Christian Louboutin sneakers with the studs on the tip. Everything in him wanted to bring her body close to his and suck her bottom lip into his mouth. Cheeko appreciated a woman who took pride in her appearance and every time he saw Suki, he could tell she did. His face may have been stoic, but his mind was everything but.

Suki realized he hadn't said anything about her remark. She caught his eyes gliding over her body and her breath caught in her throat. When he noticed he had been caught, he gave her a smirk.

"Would you like for me to put a shirt on?" Cheeko finally questioned.

"No." Suki shook her head. "This is your house. You should be comfortable." Cheeko nodded in understanding.

"Speaking of comfortable, you can take your shoes off while I go and check on the food."

Suki was so wrapped up in her thoughts she hadn't even noticed the smell of food. In his presence, all her senses were shot, but the moment he mentioned the food, she could smell it in the air.

"I should be back in here in about ten minutes. The remote is over there and you can pick from any of the movies I have on there."

"Okay."

With that, Cheeko left Suki alone to do as he said while he headed to the kitchen. Doing as she was told, Suki kicked off her sneakers and sat her Celine bag on the table. With socked feet, Suki padded toward the comfortable looking, plush theater chairs. The chairs resembled lounge chairs more than traditional recliners. Suki timidly stroked the material, and the softness instantly caught her attention. Not wasting any more time, she took a seat and sank into the material. The chair was spacious, and Suki could see herself falling asleep if she got comfortable enough.

Picking up the remote, Suki brought the screen to life and sure enough, just as Cheeko said, there was a massive selection of movies to choose from. Movies dating back as far as the '50s to the newest movies that just left theaters. It took her a little browsing before she saw one of her favorite movies. Just as she finished queuing the movie, Cheeko returned to the room with a heavenly aroma accompanying him.

"I hope you like lasagna," Cheeko commented.

Cheeko was carrying two plates with the pasta on them, with bread sticks and two bottles of water tucked under his arm.

"I love lasagna, actually," Suki confessed.

"Good."

Careful not to burn her, Cheeko handed Suki the plate before going to set his own plate down on another chair. Offering her the bottle of water, Suki gratefully accepted it before putting it in the cup holder.

"Give me a second to grab the bowls of salad and the dinner trays so you can eat comfortably."

"Do you need any help?" Suki asked, getting ready to stand up.

"Nah, you good, shorty. Just sit back and let me serve you," Cheeko told her with a wink.

Suki's heart fluttered at his words. She knew he most likely didn't mean it the way it came out, but her heart swooned all the same. Jinx had never offered to serve her or to take care of her any other way other than financially or sexually. Suki knew it wasn't logical to compare the two, but she couldn't help it. In a short amount of time, Cheeko was showing her everything her husband wasn't and everything he most likely would never be. He had been doing it since day one and his simple communication with her throughout the day, showed the major contrast between the two.

"You alright?" Cheeko asked, pulling her from her thoughts.

Suki hadn't even noticed he had stepped back in the room

as she stared off into space. Cheeko's eyes looked down at her in concern, causing her to offer him a small smile.

"I'm fine," Suki reassured.

Cheeko looked as if he didn't believe her but didn't push any further. Instead, he sat the bowls of salad on his chair before he opened the dinner tray and set it up in front of her. Once it was sturdy, Cheeko gently reached over and took the plate from her lap to place it on top of the tray and gave her the bowl of salad.

"Is Caesar okay?"

"It's perfect." Suki offered him a smile, nodding.

"Bet."

Moving out of her personal space, Cheeko moved to the side and set his tray up the same way before getting comfortable and looking up at the screen. Suki watched as his eyebrows dipped slightly and began talking.

"I know how it looks but it's a really good movie. It's one of my favorites actually," Suki began explaining. "It's not in English, so I hope you don't mind reading subtitles."

Cheeko didn't answer right away but looked at her for a moment with an expression Suki couldn't quite read.

"But if you want to watch something else, we definitely can," Suki offered quickly, getting nervous. "Not everyone is into these types of movies, and I should have thought about something more neutral," Suki rambled.

A smile spread across Cheeko's face. He thought her babbling was cute.

"Nah, this good," Cheeko told her. "I was looking like that because this is actually one of my favorite movies," he admitted.

Suki's eyes stretched as she returned his smile.

"Really? What you know about my boy Jaguar Paw?" Suki exclaimed.

"Nah, better question is, what you know about my boy?" Cheeko shot back. "This ain't no chick flick type movie."

"Who said I was into chick flicks?" Suki scrunched her nose up.

Her face was twisted in a way that showed Cheeko she was dead serious. A smooth chortle escaped his lips.

"You're right," Cheeko told her, throwing his hands up in mock surrender. "I just assumed."

"Hmph. You know what they say about assuming," Suki pointed out.

"Alright, calm down, Rocky. I don't want no smoke," Cheeko joked, earning him a playful eye roll.

Shaking her head, Suki used the small silence that fell over them as a chance to take a bite of the lasagna he brought her. The smell was causing her stomach to growl, and she knew if it got any louder, he was going to hear it. Suki's lips wrapped around the fork and her eyes instantly closed as a moan escaped her throat.

"Oh my gosh. This is so good," Suki commented after she swallowed.

"Oh yeah?" Cheeko questioned with a raised eyebrow before taking a bite of his own food. "It's not as good as my OG's but I tried to follow her recipe as best I could."

Suki's head snapped in his direction, and Cheeko was once again laughing at her because of the bewildered look on her face.

"What?" he questioned, forking more of his food.

"You cooked this?" Suki questioned in disbelief.

"What, you thought I threw it in the oven from a box?"

"I mean, yeah."

"Nah. I ain't a chef or nothing but I can hold my own in the kitchen," he told her.

"I would have never guessed," Suki commented, eating more of her food.

"I guess we both learned something surprising about the other today," Cheeko offered.

"I guess we did," Suki agreed with a smile.

No more words were spoken between the two as they ate their food. Cheeko had a mind to turn the movie on, but the silence between them wasn't uncomfortable in the slightest. He could tell Suki had relaxed completely and he was happy she felt safe enough to relax in his presence. When he had decided to text her earlier in the day, he hadn't planned to invite her over but the more they texted back and forth, he got an overwhelming urge to be around her. Same as before.

Cheeko stopped eating and allowed himself to watch Suki as she enjoyed her food. He took the time to study her movements as she took small bites of her food and chewed. She had her feet tucked underneath her as she enjoyed her meal. He could tell she wasn't eating to be cute. Her body language told him she was being herself and Cheeko could appreciate it. Suki must have sensed his eyes on her because she turned in his direction, with food stuffed in her cheeks.

She continued to chew her food and swallowed before she offered him any words.

"Is there something on my face or something?" she questioned, bringing her hand up to wipe the side of her plump lips. Cheeko had the overwhelming urge to kiss her again but resisted.

"No."

"Then why are you staring at me like that?"

"You're just beautiful to me, Suki," he admitted.

He watched as her breath hitched in her throat as she visibly gulped. His intention wasn't to make her uncomfortable, but Cheeko wasn't afraid to share his thoughts with her.

"I am?" Her voice was barely above a whisper.

"Yes. You can't see it in my eyes when I look at you?"

"Now that you mention it, every time I've been around you, I always catch you looking but your face is always so unreadable."

"Would you like to know what I was thinking?" Cheeko questioned, his voice dropping an octave.

Suki didn't miss the rugged edge his voice had taken. It was the same way he spoke in her ear as he brought her to an earth-shattering orgasm in the middle of his VIP section. His eyes bore into her, and Suki could hear her heart beating in her ears as her heart hammered in her chest and all of the blood in her body rushed to her clit.

Clearing her throat, Suki adverted her eyes from his and tried to get her hormones under control. There was no reason this man should have this type of effect on her.

"Umm, if you want to," Suki replied, unsure.

Cheeko smirked at her shyness but didn't say anything more. He could see the internal battle she was having. Not wanting to push her any further, Cheeko decided to leave the conversation alone as he stood and gathered his dishes.

"You done?" Cheeko questioned.

"Yes."

"Alright."

He simply gathered the plates and moved them to the side with the trays. He could feel her nervousness return and Cheeko wanted to kick himself for pushing her. Simone always told him that not everyone knew how to take his upfront attitude and in this moment, he was seeing how true her words were. After he had cleared the space, he went back to his chair and told Suki to start the movie.

Once the movie got underway, Suki was her normal self. She sat and watched the movie as if she had never seen it before. Cheeko had never been a fan of anyone talking during movies. It usually annoyed him to no end but watching Suki's excitement, he realized it didn't bother him when she did. Halfway through the movie, Cheeko realized Suki's commentary began to slow down and looked over to see her curled up in her chair with eyes closed.

"Suki?" Cheeko called softly.

When she didn't respond, he noticed the small rise and fall of her body signaling she had fallen asleep. Abandoning his own seat, Cheeko walked over to where she slept and watched her for a moment. Her face was scrunched ever so slightly. Squatting in front of her, her brushed her curly mane where it was falling in her face. Cheeko stroked her hair when she moved slightly. Cheeko thought she would wake up but instead, her face smoothed out and the wrinkles across her nose disappear. She visibly relaxed under his touch. Cheeko didn't want to disturb her sleep, but he also didn't want to leave her curled up in a chair, regardless of how comfortable it was.

Standing back to his feet, Cheeko leaned down before gently scooping Suki in his arms. She stirred slightly but simply cuddled to his chest before relaxing again. Careful not to tousle her too much, Cheeko walked her out of the theater room and down the hall to his bedroom. He could have simply put her in his guest bedroom but decided against it. Laying her on top of his comforter, Cheeko exited the room before returning a few seconds later with a blanket from his hall closet. Draping it over her body, Suki snuggled until his pillows but didn't wake.

Closing the door up behind him, Cheeko went to clean up the mess they had made and turn the movie off. As Cheeko gathered everything, the sound of a phone vibrating to the side caught his attention. Sitting the dishes back down, Cheeko walked over to where it sat and realized it was Suki's phone.

Picking it up, Cheeko figured he should take it to her. Glancing down at the screen, Cheeko stopped in his steps as he noticed the message. He didn't want to invade her privacy, but the words caught his attention.

HUSBAE

Sorry babe. Need to push back our movie night later. Something important came up. Can't get away. Don't wait up. Luv you.

Cheeko stared at the message for a few more seconds before pressing the power button to make the screen go back black. For a split second, Cheeko had allowed himself to entertain the idea that he and Suki could be something more. Build something more. But the message burst whatever dream bubble Cheeko found himself him. Suki wasn't his. She never would be.

CHAPTER TWELVE

Two weeks.
Two weeks of no communication.
Two weeks of no touching.
Two weeks of no Nahzir.

Simone had been trying to throw herself into work and convince herself his absence wasn't bothering her, but she knew all too well it was a lie. It wasn't like her and Nahz hadn't gotten into arguments before and had even went time without speaking because they were both being stubborn, but never this long. This time felt different. It felt *permanent.*

Chewing on the tip of her pen, Simone glanced at the clock for what felt like the millionth time in the past ten minutes. Simone didn't have a set schedule for working but she had prided herself on staying at work like the rest of the employees in the building until the work day was over. Even if her brother owned the place, Simone didn't want him to get disgruntled workers thinking he gave her special treatment. Any other day, the remaining thirty minutes of her shift wouldn't have bothered her, but today it was driving her insane.

Reluctantly bringing her eyes back to her desktop, Simone continued to work on the spreadsheets on her screen. Simone was finally getting into a groove when she noticed figures walking past the glass exterior of her office. A few workers smiled and waved at her as they headed home for the day. It took all of Simone's willpower not to spring up and run full speed out of the office in her YSL heels. Keeping her composure, Simone stood slowly and began gathering her items so she could leave for the day.

It was a little after six in the evening and she knew Nahz probably hadn't made it home yet. She had enough time to grab food before heading home to shower and get changed out of her clothes. Simone usually wasn't the first to cave when the two were on the outs, but she was tired of waiting for Nahz to reach out to her. If Simone was being honest with herself, she had to admit, she was the reason behind their current situation, but Simone wasn't sure how to fix it. In her eyes Nahz was being unreasonable with his demands. Things had been going fine for them thus far without any problems, and she didn't understand why he was so eager to change it.

The ride to her house was silent as her mind wondered how she could get Nahz to talk to her and see things her way. Simone wasn't ready to tell Cheeko of their relationship and she wanted Nahz to respect the fact that she would tell him once she was ready. Pulling into her subdivision, Simone gazed up as trees rustled in the wind sending a light breeze through her cracked window and giving her a natural background noise to calm her racing thoughts.

Simone's body moved on autopilot once she was in the confines of her home. Every day was the same routine. Come home. Eat. Shower. Look through proposals Cheeko sent her until she had her glass of wine before bed. Placing her handbag and iPad on the countertop, Simone stood at her island, her eyes taking in her surroundings. There was no noise other than the babbling water from the filter on her fish tank. Just beautiful cream-colored walls with a plush heather gray sectional and paintings on the wall. The small wall art, knick knacks, and plants gave her three-bedroom townhouse a very peaceful vibe. To anyone who entered they would feel the tranquil atmosphere that always smelled of fresh baked cookies and cinnamon, thanks to her favorite candles from Bath and Body Works. They would see a home but to Simone, it was a lifeless crypt.

Snapping herself out of her thoughts, Simone followed her nightly routine, trying her hardest to keep her mind off her pending conversation with Nahz. Before Simone realized it, the time had reached a little past ten at night and she knew she could no longer hold off on what she needed to do.

The drive to his place would get her on his doorstep a little before eleven. Allowing her mind to roam to all the things she needed to say, the only thought crushing to the front of Simone's brain was how much she missed him. Not the sex. Not all the nasty things he did to her body every time they were behind closed doors, but him specifically. As the building came into view, Simone released a breath she didn't know she was holding.

Parking her car in its usual spot, Simone gripped the steering wheel as her heart hammered in her chest. For the life of her, she couldn't seem to catch her breath. Her nerves were getting the best of her, and Simone had never had that reaction when it came to Nahz before.

"What are you, Simone? Fifteen?" Simone scolded out loud. "The worst thing he can do is turn you away. You got this."

The mini pep talk was enough to allow Simone to leave the

comfort of her car and make the small trek up the stairs that led to his door. Music could be heard from down the hall and the closer she got, Simone realized the music was coming from behind his door. Knitting her manicured eyebrows together, Simone raised her hand to knock. She could have called or texted, but Simone didn't want to risk the chance of him ignoring her again. Now she was here, and he would have to face her whether he wanted to or not.

When no one came to the door, Simone raised her fist and began to knock harder. She knew she may have been inconsiderate, but her patience was beginning to wear thin. On the other side of the door, Simone heard faint footsteps coming toward the door over the sound of the music on the other side. The locks began to slide out of place and Simone took a deep breath, fully prepared to give him a piece of her mind.

Instinctively closing her eyes, Simone felt the breeze come from the other side of the door as it was opened, and music spilled out. Simone knew if she saw his face and how good he looked, she wouldn't want to talk, she'd want him to take her body in whatever way he wanted. If he wanted it fast, she would give it to him. If he wanted it slow to punish her for the way she had been acting, Simone would gladly take it too. If he wanted to tie her down and fuck some sense into her to let off his frustrations, Simone would happily obliged. But Simone knew that could come after she said what she had to say. As bad as she didn't want to, she knew she needed to apologize, and the only way to do that was avoiding eye contact for a moment.

"I know you call yourself having an attitude and you don't want to talk right now, but I'm tired of this shit, Nahzir. Either be a man and talk to me or don't, but I'm not going to keep chasing you. But I also can't leave things up in the air the way they are," Simone rushed out. "Look, I know I was wrong for the way I've been going about things, and you haven't been handling them any better with your temper tantrum."

"Oh honey." The light airy voice of a female had Simone's head snapping up and her eyes following. "I could never be the one to pull what you just did but you got heart, I give you that," the girl commented with a shake of her head.

Simone's eyes were glued to her face, and the sinking pit in her stomach seemed to be non-ending. Simone stood with her mouth opening and closing, not being able to form the words. Her eyes jetted to the side, and she took a step back, confusion etched on her face as she made sure she had come to the right place. Surely, this had to be a mistake.

1522.

Nope. No mistake. This was Nahzir's house and there was a woman on the other side in the space he occupied.

"Yo, Shawnie. Who was at the door?" The sound of his smooth baritone getting closer caused Simone to look further into the house.

Simone noticed his bare chest and the basketball shorts hanging loosely from his hips. From where she stood, she could tell he wasn't wearing underwear. Allowing her eyes to go back to who he had called Shawnie, for the first time, Simone noticed she was only wearing a t-shirt that swallowed her slender frame and stopped just under her ass cheeks. It wasn't just any shirt though. It was his shirt. Shawnie's hair was tousled slightly as if she had just jumped out the bed.

Simone's heart clattered loudly in her chest. The feeling of it literally being torn apart caused her to take a step back as if she had been stabbed.

Why was this woman here? Who was she? Did she mean something to him or was she some random hookup?

So many thoughts whirled around in her head but none of

them seemed to formulate out her mouth. For once, Simone was speechless.

"Nahzir, this woman came to see you," Shawnie explained. "I think you should talk to her."

"Nahzir," Simone repeated softly.

A name only associated with those close to him fell from her lips. Not even Cheeko called Nahz by his first name. If he allowed her to call him something so intimate, then they must be close. She must be special. This woman was different.

Simone watched as his fingers curled the door before it was pulled completely open and his mouth opened so he could speak, but the moment his eyes landed on her, Simone could see the surprise register in his eyes for a split second. Clearing his throat, Nahz's face was completely stoic.

"Yo, Mone," Nahz called out. "What you doing here? You know how late it is?"

The way the words effected Simone, she felt as if she was smacked in the face.

"What am I?" Simone started softly, her words trailing off. Eyes still bouncing between him and the woman standing next to him.

Noticing where her eyes were roaming, Nahz glanced down at Shawnie before speaking.

"Aye, give me a minute."

Rolling her eyes in her head, Shawnie's body language showed she didn't want to leave Nahz with Simone. Probably not after what she had heard, but she didn't put up a fight. She simply backed away and took light steps away from the door. Nahz watched her until she disappeared before turning his eyes back toward Simone.

"Who is she?" Simone questioned, her voice not yet back at normal volume.

Being soft spoken was nothing like her. She never talked

low. She was always outspoken, but now? Now, Simone couldn't seem to find her voice. She felt it sinking with her heart. This was like having the nightmare where you fell, and you would give anything to wake up but you couldn't. Simone was falling and screaming, and no words were coming out. She desperately wanted to wake up.

"Simone." His voice was all but a groan.

Nahz's face never changed and his voice was laced with annoyance, as if Simone wasn't wanted.

"Nahzir. Who. Is. She?" Each word was broken up falling from her lips.

She didn't want to ask again, but fuck! What else was she supposed to ask? Every reason Simone had made this drive no longer mattered. They had bigger problems at hand.

Brushing a hand down the front of his waves, Nahz glanced over his shoulder before stepping further outside and pulling the door up behind him. Nahz wanted to be anywhere but having this conversation, but now he was here. There was no running.

Silence fell between the pair as Simone studied his face. Desperate was a word she would never use to describe herself but in this moment of time, she was. Desperate for answers. Desperate to know who this woman was. Just desperate.

"Who—" Simone began, ready to question again.

"Does it matter, Simone?" Nahz questioned, his harsh words cutting off anything that came from her lips. "Why does it matter who she is?"

Taken aback by his sudden attitude, Simone didn't know whether she wanted to slap him for snapping at her or curse him out.

"It matters because I want to know!" Simone replied.

"And again, why? You don't have no right questioning me about what I do or who I stick my dick in, shorty. You made it clear you don't want me, but it's a problem now that you see someone else does?" Nahz scoffed. "What you expected, huh? I was going to be here sitting on my hands waiting on you to come back around like I always do? Or did you expect me to chase you because you think a nigga is just weak for you? Or wait, did you think you were going to come here, bat your eyelashes, and I was going to fuck you senseless, and all would be forgiven?

"Nah. I told you I was done, and I meant that shit. I'm not some toy you can pick up and put down when you feel like it, Simone! So again, what the fuck are you doing here? 'Cause to be real, shorty, I ain't got shit for you."

Venom laced his words as his face never showed any true emotion. Tears stung Simone's eyes as her eyes trailed his body. This wasn't the man she had fallen in love with. This was someone completely new, and from the way he spoke, Simone knew this was a monster of her creating. Instead of replying, Simone's feet began to back away from him. She wanted to be anywhere but here. Turning around abruptly, Simone's feet carried her away from his doorstep. Her vision was blurred, and her throat burned from her holding back the sobs clawing to escape.

"Simone!"

She heard him call her name, but she had to get away. She couldn't stand there and listen to any more. Her heart couldn't take it. He was right. Simone had no right questioning him. Finally in the seclusion of her car, the wail that escaped Simone's throat caused her body to shake and tears flowed freely down her cheeks. Nahz was right, over the past couple weeks Simone had thought all those things. She had played games with his heart and ultimately lost; and now, he was done with her. For good.

CHAPTER THIRTEEN

Scrubbing his hand over his tired face, Jinx tried to wake himself up as his eyes fell back on the numbers on the elevator. For the past four days, Jinx felt as if shit just kept getting piled in his lap. After his meeting with Hector, Jinx thought he had a little more time before he would have to see who Hector had chosen over him, but he wasn't so lucky. Hector had called first thing that morning and informed Jinx he expected him to meet his new business associates tomorrow afternoon.

On top of the fact he just wasn't in the mood to do it, Jinx had too much other shit on his mind. His construction company had suddenly lost the permit for a major project because the developers hit a snag and now, he had been back and forth to the hospital the past three days. The only saving grace in all of this was Suki wasn't giving him any issues. Since Jinx had given Suki the freedom to go back to work, she had been completely focused. Most days, she made it home around the same time he did so Jinx never had to worry about being questioned about where he was.

The elevator door opened and Jinx stepped off, headed in the direction of the room he had grown accustomed to. His feet were on auto pilot as Jinx's mind ran rampant. He was running off five hours of sleep and all Jinx wanted to do was go lay in his bed, but he knew that wasn't an option. After he left here, he had to swing by his office building before running to city hall and praying he could figure out what was going on. Jinx didn't want to lose out on the million-dollar contract that was only in the developing stages. Jinx had every plan to bring Suki along so she could offer her interior design skills to the owners once everything was up and running. Jinx needed his hand in all the cookie jars.

Without knocking, Jinx pushed the hospital room door open and stepped further inside. His eyes fell to Marina as she lay in the hospital bed watching some show on TV. When she felt his presence, she turned to him with a smile on her face.

"How's my girl doing today?" Jinx questioned, stepping further into the room.

"Me or your daughter?" Marina questioned with a smirk.

"Both," Jinx replied smoothly. Walking closer to her bed, Jinx dropped a kiss on the top of Marina's head before placing a hand on her stomach.

With Suki coming back home, Jinx had placed Marina on the back burner so he wouldn't have any distractions. When Suki had started staying in the guest room and had made it clear she had no plans on fucking with him, Jinx felt it was only right for him to focus on home. And he was right. Suki had eventually come around and had even been sexing him more regularly. Jinx knew he wouldn't have accomplished that feat if he had still been dropping by Marina's to see his boys before letting her empty his nut sack.

In the midst of him ignoring her, however, Marina almost miscarried from the stress and had been placed on bed rest and hospital stay until the doctors were sure she and the baby would be safe. The doctors had made the suggestion she would be able to be discharged sooner if she had someone to go home to. Marina needed around the clock care until the baby was born and Jinx just couldn't offer that to her. He was already risking visiting her every day, sometimes twice a day, but he'd do anything for his child. Jinx was a lot of things, but he prided himself on being a good father to his kids. Even the unborn ones.

"We're doing good," Marina answered. "I thought you were coming a little bit later on."

"I was but I got a lot to do today so I came while I had the time," Jinx told her. "Has the doctor already come and checked on you today?"

"Yeah. She made her rounds about an hour ago. She said I'm not having any contractions but she doesn't feel comfortable sending me home without someone there with me and the boys."

Jinx heard the suggestion in her voice and he had to stop himself from blowing out a sigh. Jinx knew Marina wanted him to commit to being at her house daily, but she knew just as well as he did that it wasn't possible.

"Don't start, Marina," Jinx warned.

"I'm just saying what she told me, Jinx," Marina huffed with an eyeroll, folding her arms across her chest.

"And I heard when she said it the first day," Jinx shot back.

Marina glared at him where he sat.

"I just don't understand what's so hard about it."

Jinx scoffed and sat back in his chair with his hands folded neatly on his lap as he stared at her. Jinx wasn't sure if the pregnancy was fucking with her brain cells or if she was seriously suggesting he move in with her knowing he had a wife at home.

"What do you think, Marina? What about this situation is easy?" Jinx questioned sarcastically.

Rolling her eyes, Marina matched his stare.

"You don't have to be such an asshole about it."

"I'm not being an asshole. I'm asking a genuine question. What about this situation do you feel is so easy that I can uproot my life and move with you, knowing my situation?"

"I don't even know why you're still there. You're not even in love with her," Marina accused.

"And how you figure that?" Jinx questioned with a raised brow.

"Because if you were, she would be laying in this hospital bed struggling to keep your baby alive in her stomach, not me!" Marina snapped, her chest rising and falling rapidly.

The sound of the monitors began to raise a little and Jinx realized he was doing one of the things the doctors and nurses warned him were bad for Marina and the baby, stressing her out. Letting out a heavy sigh, Jinx leaned forward and rested his elbows on his knees.

"You need to calm down before you hurt her," Jinx replied lowly.

"She's already hurt, Jinx!" Marina exclaimed. "Look at where we are!"

Silence fell over the room as Jinx stared at her. As much as he wanted to wrap his fingers around her throat for the way she was talking to him, he understood her frustration. Here she was lying in a hospital bed, lonely day in and day out while he went home to his wife every night. It wasn't as if Marina didn't know what she signed up for when she committed to being his side chick and having his babies, but he could understand her frustrations. Marina wanted Jinx to give her what he was giving Suki, and he couldn't. He thought she understood that, but he must've guessed wrong.

"Look, Marina," Jinx started, but the ringing of his phone stopped his sentence.

Digging into his pocket, Jinx pulled it out and cursed immediately at the sight of the name on the screen. Checking the clock on the wall, he saw it was her lunchtime and she was probably calling to check in with him. Giving Marina a hard look, Jinx slide the cursor on the phone, allowing it to connect.

"Hold on, baby. Let me step somewhere quieter," Jinx spoke into the phone. Standing to his feet, he stepped into the bathroom inside Marina's room before placing the phone back to his ear.

"I'm back."

"Hey babe. I was seeing if you wanted to grab a bite to eat. I have a longer lunch today since I don't have to meet my next client until a little after two."

Jinx closed his eyes. He knew he wouldn't be able to make it, and to tell her yet again he wouldn't be able to caused Jinx to silently curse himself out. He hadn't been able to make up missing their movie night to her in light of everything else he had going on, and Jinx could see himself sliding further and further back into the doghouse.

"I can't today, baby," Jinx finally spoke. "After this meeting, I have to run to city hall then meet with the developers to see what I can do before I lose this contract altogether. I'm going to be wrapped up for most of the afternoon."

"Oh." Jinx could hear the disappointment in Suki's voice. "Well, what time is the meeting?"

"The one at city hall?"

"Yeah."

"Around three," Jinx replied. "Why?"

"Well after I leave from eating, I could swing by and bring you some takeout. Since it doesn't seem like you're going to get a chance to do any of that today with your schedule."

"You ain't gotta do that, baby," Jinx told her, nervousness setting in his bones. He truly did have a meeting with city hall so it wasn't a lie, but he had told his office he wouldn't be in today until after his meeting, so her showing up would get him caught in a lie.

"It's okay, I don't mind," Suki told him.

"Look, how about this," Jinx started, "Instead of you bringing me food today, how about I just take you out to your favorite restaurant on Saturday? I been planning to make it up to you and it was supposed to be a surprise."

Jinx held his breath as silence filled the other end.

When too much time passed, Jinx's nervousness began to turn into dread. He truly wasn't trying to be back on bad terms with Suki again, but he knew it would be nearly impossible to make it from the hospital back to his office at this time of day.

"Suk—" Jinx started.

"My favorite restaurant?" Suki questioned. "And I can order anything I want?"

Jinx released the breath he was holding.

"Yep. Anything you want, baby girl," Jinx told her.

"Okay, fine." She gave in. "But I'll still bring you home dessert."

A smile split across Jinx's face and he was silently thanking the universe Suki fed into his bullshit. Now all he had to do was pull some strings and make a reservation or he'd be in deep shit.

"Alright baby."

"Okay, good. I'll let you get back to work."

"See you at home tonight, baby."

"Okay. See you then."

"I love you Suki," Jinx called out.

There was a brief pause from Suki.

"I love you too. Bye."

Hanging up the phone, Jinx looked in the small mirror on the wall and just stared at his reflection. He had to get a grip on his life. Everything seemed to be spiraling out of control, and Jinx would be damned if he didn't come out on top.

Bracing himself for the bullshit he knew awaited him on the other side of the door, Jinx walked back into Marina's room to find her staring a hole in his direction. Fuck being outlined in white chalk, if looks could kill, he knew Marina would have put one between his eyes without a second thought.

"Just don't, Marina," Jinx told her before any words could fall out of her mouth.

"Don't what, Jinx?" Marina rebutted. "Don't curse you out for disrespecting me? Or don't curse you out for the pure audacity you have to answer the phone for your bitch of a wife in my face before sneaking off to tell her you love her? Please tell me, Jinx, what *don't* you want me to do at this moment?"

Before Marina had a chance to blink, Jinx was invading her space, squeezing her cheeks together. Jinx watched the anger in her eyes as he tightened his grip, ready to break her jaw for the shit she let fly out of her mouth.

"Watch your fucking mouth, Marina," Jinx gritted.

"Or what?"

The question came out muddled because of the way Jinx was holding her face, but the defiance never left her eyes. Letting her face go with a shove, Jinx straightened his body up as he glared down at her.

"I'm going to leave before I catch a DV charge against your stupid ass," Jinx commented.

The two sat having a staring contest for a few more seconds before Jinx headed to leave out of the room. As if he remembered something, Jinx stopped a few steps away from the door before facing Marina again.

"I don't know what you got going on Marina, but I suggest

you fix it. Disrespect my wife again, and me squeezing your cheeks will be the last thing you got to worry about. I'll make your ass a memory and that *bitch*, as you call her, will be the only mother my kids remember," Jinx warned.

Jinx's threat was cleared. The deadliness in his eyes spoke volumes.

"Oh, and I won't be back until Sunday. Fix your attitude before then," Jinx added.

Without another word, Jinx left the hospital room ready to put as much distance between him and Marina as possible. Jinx felt it in his bones from the look in her eyes, she was about to become a problem. But Jinx meant what he said. He'd have to find a way to make it work, but he'd kill Marina and have Suki raising his kids as if they were her own. Suki leaving him wasn't an option. He showed her that when she pulled it the first time and if push came to shove, he'd show her a side of him she'd never seen. Jinx just hoped that wasn't the case because he'd hate to have to lose both his bitches because one of them wanted to be bitter.

CHAPTER FOURTEEN

Marina sat seething well after Jinx had left her hospital room. How dare he threaten her as if she meant nothing to him? Pulling a pillow over her face, Marina screamed to let out her frustration. She had done so much planning over the past few weeks trying to find a way to make Jinx come back to her. All her planning did was lead her into a hospital room where she was confined to bed. When she had called her best friend to help her out with her plan, Marina felt it was fool proof. If Jinx saw her on the verge of losing his first daughter, he would come running to be at her side.

And yes, it worked to an extent, but not to the extent Marina wanted it to. Pulling the pillow from over her head, Marina stared up at the dots on the ceiling as she tried to find a way to get Jinx to see things her way. Light taps came at her room door and Marina sat up, forcing the fake smile she had been wearing since she came here on her face.

"Come in," Marina called out.

She expected one of the doctors or nurses to be coming in

to bother her like they always did, but when Marina saw it was only her best friend, she allowed the smile to drop from her face.

"Oh, it's only you."

"Only me? Bitch, don't do that," her best friend Toi huffed. "I just saw your baby daddy getting on the elevator and he looked like he was ready to mob on a bitch," Toi joked with a wave of her head. "What'd you do this time?"

"Why do you always feel like I did something?" Marina questioned with a snarl.

Toi gave her a knowing look as she sat down in the chair Jinx occupied earlier and placed a bag on the table Marina hadn't noticed she was carrying. The smell of food wafted into Marina's nose and her stomach instantly growled audibly. She was so tired of eating hospital food and if she would have known Jinx was coming, she would have made him stop to grab her something.

"Don't worry greedy, I got something for you and fat mama in here," Toi told her, putting the containers on the bed tray and pulling her chair up.

Marina watched Toi in her scrubs as she set up the containers, and Marina caught herself looking at the diamond ring that adorned her left hand. A small tinge of jealously panged in Marina's heart, because what was so special about Toi that she was able to be married to the man of her dreams while Marina played second fiddle? Toi was pretty and her body was snatched, but that was all. Yeah, she had a couple of degrees, and she worked her ass off to get herself through nursing school, but the moment she met her husband, Toi could have sat back and kicked her feet up.

Not only did Toi's husband adore her but he was fine and paid with a good ass job. The man was a fucking neurosurgeon for Pete's sake, and Toi still decided to work in the hospital when she didn't have to. If Marina was in her shoes, she would have been putting in her notice before the ink was dry on the marriage certificate.

"So, are you going to tell me why you look as if you got laser beams coming out of your eyes?" Toi questioned, handing the container of Chinese food to Marina.

"Because I'm so sick of that nigga playing in my face as if I don't matter," Marina seethed. "Can you believe he had the nerve to step into the bathroom and tell that bitch that he loved her while I'm laying here? And it wasn't an *I love you too* moment. He said it first."

"I mean, what did you expect, Rina? That is his wife," Toi reasoned.

"As if I need one more person reminding me who the fuck she is!"

"Hey, don't get mad at me. I'm just saying."

"Yeah, whatever," Marina mumbled.

Eating a couple of spoonfuls of her food, Marina watched Toi silently, trying to figure out a way to approach what she wanted to ask.

"I need your help again," Marina blurted out.

"Oh no," Toi said, shaking her head. "Look where my *help* got you this time," Toi spoke, gesturing around the hospital room.

"I know, but it wasn't enough."

"Of course, it wasn't enough. Did you seriously think I was going to let you talk me into giving you a whole bag of Oxytocin to jump start your labor? You're already laid up in a hospital on bed rest until you deliver because you keep having contractions from the small dosage I gave you."

"I know Toi, but he still treats me like shit," Marina argued. "I thought it would be enough for him to see with me and his kids is where he needs to be, but no. He's still out running behind that bitch."

"Then maybe it's time you opened your eyes. If you damn near forced yourself to go into preterm labor once to get his attention and he still curving you, then what makes you think he's going to come the second time if you did it again?"

Marina heard everything Toi was trying to say, but she wasn't the least bit interested. Toi would never understand because she had the man of her dreams. Couldn't she see that Marina was only trying to get hers?

"Are you going to help me or not, Toi?" Marina questioned with a straight face.

"No! Hell no, I'm not helping you!" Toi exclaimed. "The only reason I agreed to help you the first time is because I owed you for the ten grand you gave me while I was in school, and you wanted to pull that bullshit IOU card. I could lose my fucking license if they found out what I did."

"I mean, you could lose your license if someone told them what you did too," Marina shot back with a shrug.

Toi's eyes narrowed into slits as she stared at her best friend. In all the years they'd been friends, Toi had seen Marina cross many people to get what she wanted, but Toi never thought in a million years that she'd be in her eyesight.

"Are you fucking serious right now?"

"Do I look like I'm playing?"

"You're a low-down dirty bitch, you know that?"

Marina simply shrugged. This was nothing new, and if Toi thought name calling was going to get Marina to change her mind, then she was sadly mistaken. She wanted what she wanted, and she would sacrifice anyone to get it. It wasn't her fault Toi let slip the one way Marina could blackmail her into doing what she wanted. Marina was prepared to pay Toi off if need be, but learning she could lose the career she loved so much and it would cost Marina nothing was priceless.

"They have a special place in hell for people like you," Toi commented, wiping the tears that sprang into her eyes. "I hope this nigga is worth you possibly losing your life and the life of your child if shit goes wrong. And if it does, remember I won't be there to save you."

"Yeah, yeah. Save all the dramatics," Marina spoke, waving her off. "When can you get it to me?"

Scoffing, Toi shook her head and wiped her dripping nose. She couldn't believe this shit, but she should have known better.

"You'll have to wait until the weekend when the hospital is less busy. And after this Marina, lose my fucking number and never call me ever the fuck again. Because when this shit blows up in your face, and it will, I won't be around to bail you out like I always am."

Marina watched as Toi stormed out of her room. Toi would get over it and if she didn't, fuck her. But she was right, Jinx was worth that much to her. Picking back up her food, the first genuine smile since she'd been there ended up spreading across Marina's face. She was one step closer to securing her man and if she did lose their daughter, it would still get Marina what she wanted because he'd blame himself. In Marina's eyes, it was a win-win situation.

CHAPTER FIFTEEN

Suki looked over her shoulder as her heels clicked across the pavement. When she was satisfied no one was watching her as she left the office building, she turned back around and scanned the parking lot. When she spotted the cream white Rolls Royce sitting on the far end of the parking lot, a smile hit her lips and she picked up her pace. Bypassing the front door, Suki stopped in the front of the back door as instructed before she pulled the door open and stooped down to get inside.

As she sank into the peanut butter seats, the smell of Dior Sauvage filled Suki's nose and caused her clit to thump. Turning to the side, the sight of Cheeko caused her smile to grow.

"Damn," Cheeko greeted. "I thought you looked good as fuck dressed down, but this business attire shit sexy as fuck."

A blush warmed Suki's cheeks. She had left her suit jacket in her office and had opted to come out in her navy-blue pencil skirt with the white button-down shirt paired with nude red bottoms on her feet.

"Thank you." Suki smiled. "You don't look half bad your-self," Suki commented, and she wasn't lying.

Suki could tell he was dressed for work. She allowed her eyes to slowly slink over Cheeko's body. The red dress pants he sported contrasted perfectly with his peanut butter complex-ion. The sleeves of his button-down shirt were rolled up, showing off his tattooed forearms. His dreads were freshly re-twisted and pulled away from his face in a low ponytail. By the time Suki's eyes made it to Cheeko's lips, she was stuck. His lips were one of her favorite parts of his body. They were so full and kissable looking.

"You just gone stare at me, or we gone eat this food before it gets cold?"

Suki's eyes snapped to meet his, and the smirk he wore told her he knew exactly what she was thinking.

"We can eat," Suki told him with a nod.

"Since we eating in the car, I decided to just get some easy choices," he told her, leaning down and pulling some food out of a bag by his feet.

"I got lamb and shrimp kebabs. Chicken and steak tacos."

"Hmmm. I'll take a lamb kebab and a steak taco."

Cheeko bobbed his head as he set everything out. Cheeko opened each container and Suki's mouth began to water.

"You better be glad I like you, because I ain't never ate in this car," Cheeko joked. "And these little ass tacos gone piss my stomach off."

"Awww. I feel special."

"You better," Cheeko told her with a smirk.

Eating their food in comfortable silence, Cheeko watched Suki as she ate her food and took in her features. Cheeko was drawn to Suki in a way he couldn't explain. Since the night at his house, Cheeko had been trying to keep his distance, but it seemed the more he tried, the stronger the pull was. He had never seen himself as the side nigga type and he wasn't ready to start now. Cheeko knew he couldn't take it further than he had at the club, but he knew he didn't want to stop dealing with her completely. Suki was the calm in his life he needed, even if he couldn't have her fully. The time they spent together over the past few weeks put Cheeko's heart at ease. If he wasn't finding a way to be in her presence, then he texted her until he fell asleep at night. Suki had him sitting on the phone one night as if he was back in middle school. He caught himself lounging in different positions all over his house just talking.

"Now, who's staring?" Suki asked in a soft voice.

"Man hush." Cheeko laughed. "Just finish eating your food."

Taking his own advice, Cheeko ate his food and allowed the music in the background to fill the silence between them. Ten minutes passed before they finished up their food and started to put their trash away.

"How long do you have before you have to go back to work?" Suki asked, her voice slicing through the air.

"I'm off for the day. I'm headed out to a business meeting with a client."

"Oh. Simone meeting you there?"

"Nah. This ain't that type of meeting. Speaking of Simone, she didn't come to work this morning. She said she wasn't feeling well," Cheeko commented.

"I'll have to check on her after I get off work." Suki pouted. "I may have to bring her some soup or something."

"Let me find out you like my sister better than me," Cheeko teased.

"Because I do," Suki rebutted, sticking her tongue out.

"Damn, it's like that?" Cheeko questioned with his hand to his chest, feigning hurt.

"Don't pout. I like you too."

"Nahh, my feelings hurt now."

"Awwww, I didn't mean to hurt your feelings," Suki told him, poking his cheek.

In one swift movement, Cheeko grabbed ahold of Suki's wrist and pulled her body toward him. Careful not to let her body hit the ground, Cheeko wrapped his other arm around her waist and set her directly in his lap.

"My feelings still hurt, you gotta make it up to me," Cheeko replied in a low voice.

"Okay." Suki's voice was barely a whisper. Her boobs were pressed into Cheeko's chest and they were practically nose to nose. Suki didn't know how he wanted her to make it up to him, but she was willing to do anything at this point. Her eyes darted to his lips again before she was staring into his brown orbs.

"How?" Suki asked.

"You know how."

Not thinking too much into it, Suki pressed her lips into Cheeko's and immediately melted into his body. His lips were everything she thought they would be and then some. The kiss started slow, like two teenagers afraid to make the wrong move. Opening his mouth, Cheeko swiped his tongue over Suki's lips, causing her to open them on contact.

Deepening the kiss, Cheeko let go of her wrist and placed his hand on the back on her neck, trapping her. A soft moan escaped her throat as she felt the stiffening of his dick against her butt. Without breaking the kiss, Cheeko adjusted to allow Suki to straddle his lap. Her hands moved frantically as she hiked the skirt up to free her legs.

Their tongues meshed together as Cheeko's hands rubbed up her thighs before resting on her bare ass. The G-string she wore allowed Cheeko to feel the heat of her center on his lap, causing his dick to strain against the fabric of his slacks.

Her lips tasted sweet even though they hadn't had any dessert. They were soft and delicate and Cheeko would give anything to see his dick sliding in and out from between them. He knew his dick would fill her lips up almost to capacity. Both sets, and Cheeko could feel the restraint he had been trying too hard to hold onto slowly slipping. The lines he had drawn in the dirt for them were fading, and he knew the moment he gave into his desire Suki would belong to him. There would be no more going home to her husband. There would be no more playing the background. She would be his and his only. Cheeko was a territorial bastard, and he would kill to protect what he felt was his, and he could see himself killing behind Suki. Every logical thought in his head was telling him to stop before he was slowly sinking Suki down onto his dick and ravishing her walls in the backseat of his Rolls Royce, but his body wouldn't listen.

Suki's fingernails raked across Cheeko's skin in the most possessive way. Not being able to help the movement, her hips began to grind against the bulge sitting perfectly between her legs. He was lined so perfectly with her pussy and Suki wanted to feel it. She *needed* to feel it.

"I want you," Suki admitted, breaking the kiss.

Suki barely recognized her own voice, pure lust and desperation dripped in her tone. She sounded the way she felt; needy.

Cheeko's eyes bore into hers as she continued to grind on his lap. His eyes closed for a second, trying to concentrate. When he opened them again, Suki was still staring at him, studying his features.

"If we do this, there's no turning back, Suk," Cheeko warned. "You understand?"

Suki head shook up and down immediately.

"No. Do you understand me? There's no going home to that nigga after this. The moment I put my dick inside you, you belong to me. I don't share, Suki. I'm selfish as fuck. You really prepared to leave everything you share with that nigga to be with me?

"Won't be no going back to get your shit. No giving explanations. The moment we do this, you become mine. That's it. You prepared for that?"

Suki's eyes furrowed slightly, and the lust-filled haze she was in slowly began to lift. Was she ready to leave Jinx completely to be with Cheeko? Yes, Jinx had his faults, but what if Cheeko had just as many?

Without another word, Cheeko began to move Suki from his lap. The uncertainty that danced in her eyes was all the confirmation Cheeko needed to see Suki didn't understand the seriousness of their situation. She wasn't ready to give up on her husband, and maybe it was unfair for him to ask her to, but for him it was all or nothing. He thought Suki understood that.

Embarrassment instantly washed over Suki as she began to straighten her clothes once Cheeko moved away from her. He didn't speak and for the first time, the silence between them wasn't comfortable. It was suffocating. Suki wanted to run and hide.

"I'm sorry, Cheeko," Suki told him, her voice barely audible, but he had heard her.

Cheeko didn't want her apology. He wanted her, but she made it crystal clear in that moment that he couldn't have her. As much as the reality stung his eyes, Cheeko had to accept in.

"You need to get back to work and I need to get to my meeting," Cheeko said, his eyes staring straight ahead.

Suki realized he hadn't responded to her apology, but what did she expect him to say? Finishing straightening her clothes, Suki made sure everything was in place before she placed her hand on the handle and opened it. A part of her wanted Cheeko to stop her, but he wouldn't even look in her direction.

When Suki noticed she wasn't going to get any more words out of him, she allowed herself to get out of the car and close the door behind her. With each step she took, Suki could feel her heart ache more and more. Cheeko wasn't her man, but she felt her heart break all the same.

Cheeko wanted something from her she couldn't give him, but the fact she wanted to is what hurt the most. Suki had exchanged vows to love Jinx for better or for worse. As a lone tear escaped the corner of her eye, Suki prayed she had made the right decision.

CHAPTER SIXTEEN

"Cheeko, my friend!"

Hector's heavy accent greeted him as he stepped into the office with Nahz.

"So glad you could make it!" Hector told him. "Nice to see you too, Nahz."

"What's up, Hector," Nahz replied.

Both men shook his hand before taking their seats. Cheeko had yet to say anything, his mind was a million miles away still in that parking lot watching Suki walk away from him. If Cheeko was a weak nigga, he would have jumped out and chased her. He would have made her see he was where she needed to be, but Cheeko wasn't weak. If a woman didn't see his worth then it wasn't his job to show her.

Suki should have been the last thing on Cheeko's mind while he was out handling business, but he couldn't help himself. Suki was like a monkey on his back.

"I don't think I've ever seen you make that face, amigo," Hector commented, breaking Cheeko's train of thought.

"Huh?"

Hector's laugh filled the room as he sat back in his chair.

"Only a woman could make someone of your talents be off your square to this degree."

"I may be a little distracted, but I'm never off my square, Hector," Cheeko corrected. "I'm simply waiting on this little meet and greet to take place. Even though if all three of us are here, there's no reason we're missing the fourth," Cheeko pointed out.

"I couldn't agree more with you, my friend, but not everyone thinks the way we do. They do not see the value of time. Which is why I chose you to be my transporter. I could have simply given my whole operation over to him and went on about my way to retirement, but I have something else in mind that suits everyone involved much better."

"And what would that be?" Cheeko questioned with a raised eyebrow.

"Later, my friend. Later." Hector waved Cheeko off, causing Cheeko to look at Nahz.

Nahz shrugged his shoulders as if it was no big deal, but Cheeko knew his man enough to know Hector's words had definitely piqued Nahz's interest as well. Men of Hector's caliber didn't simply make plans without cause, and anything Hector was about to bring to the table was a sure way for them both to make money. The only part about Hector's comment was the fact that he would willingly do business with someone he didn't deem worthy. As if Hector could read Cheeko's mind, he began speaking.

"Sometimes when you know what type of animal you are dealing with, it is better to keep them on a leash where you can control them, rather than set them free where they become a problem. Especially when that animal is unpredictable."

"Then wouldn't it be better to just put the animal down?"

Nahz chimed in. "Better to put them down now than to deal with the clean-up later."

"This is true, but when a dog is bad, you don't kill it or starve it. You simply beat it to remind it who its owner is. You show them who is dominant. Beat them enough, they will become obedient because they know who feeds them. Train them enough that once you let them off their leash, you don't have to worry about them becoming a problem. They will remain loyal regardless of whose care you entrust them to."

Cheeko was two seconds away from telling Hector to quit talking to him in riddles, when a knock on the door silenced him.

"Come," Hector called out.

The door to the office opened again, and the last person Cheeko expected to see walked through the door.

"Jinx. You're actually on time today," Hector called out. "Jinx, I would like for you to meet your new business partners and old friends of mine, Cheeko and Nahz."

All the color seemed to drain from Jinx's face as he laid eyes on the two motherfuckers he had a gun deal with a few weeks prior. When Hector mentioned he was handing all his shipments and transports over to an associate of his, the young motherfuckers in front of him were never on that list of people.

How the fuck these two know Hector?

"No need for introductions, Hector. We've met," Cheeko spoke before Jinx could.

"Oh, that's good then! Are you gentlemen in business together?" Hector asked, looking between the trio.

"We weren't, but it seems we are now."

Jinx caught the shade in Cheeko's voice, and he wanted to slap the smug look off his face. Jinx was really confused now. What could Hector have possibly been thinking putting those two in a position of power such as this and leaving him eating crumbs? This had to be some type of joke.

"Ahh. I see," Hector said. "Jinx, sit down so we can discuss business."

Jinx sat down as Hector and Cheeko talked, only responding when it was directly related to him. His mind was all over the place as he tried to figure out what was really going on. Hector seriously thought these two Rugrats could do a better job than him?

"Drop-off will stay the same, but for each late pickup or drop-off, there will be an extra ten stacks tacked on to the price. The price will move according to how many times the problem occurs," Cheeko explained, causing Jinx's ears to perk up.

"Wait. Are you seriously saying you'd charge me ten stacks for being late picking up my own shit? You can't be serious."

"Very," Cheeko commented. "It may be your product but we're on *my* time, and my time is very valuable. If you don't want to pay a fee, don't be late," Cheeko told him with a shrug.

"And Hector, you're okay with this?"

"Doesn't matter if I'm okay with it or not, these are his rules." Hector shrugged. "Same rule he's always had. I don't expect it to change now."

"Any more questions?" Cheeko asked with a raised brow.

Waving him off, Jinx sat back in his chair as Cheeko continued to talk.

"Each drop and pickup with be in a different location. The day before each pickup, you'll get a text with a time and place to meet Nahz so he can collect payment, then he will provide you with the location for the pickup along with the times and a shipment container number. You're responsible for moving your own product and getting it shipped where you need it to go. There will be a window of time where I've made that possible for you to move without issues, which is why the schedule is important.

"Anything outside of the time frame I've set, late fees and penalties will be added toward the next shipment. I already have the next three dates mapped out. Any questions?"

"Yeah, one. How old are you?" Jinx inquired.

Cheeko's brow knitted in the center before realization dawned on him. A smooth chortle escaped his throat and filled the air around him.

"Old enough to earn the trust of the men to my left and my right," Cheeko pointed out. "But if you want to know how long it's been since I finally bust my way out my mom's coochie, then the answer is twenty-eight."

"Gentlemen, no need for the penis showing contest. We stand to make a lot of money together."

Cheeko's eyes stayed on Jinx a little while longer before he began to ignore him completely. Cheeko could see now Jinx would be a problem, but he wasn't the least bit worried. Hector may not be willing to put his dog down, but Cheeko was. And he'd lose not a wink of sleep after.

———

Two days had passed since Suki had heard from Cheeko and she was beginning to feel the void. She hadn't realized how much talking to him every day had lifted her spirits until he was no longer around to do it. Suki thought that if she had given him the night to get over what had happened between them in the car, he would get over his attitude and reach out to her, but nope. She hadn't heard a peep from him.

Finally giving in, Suki had sent him a text asking him if they could talk in person that morning when she woke up, but he never responded. Checking her phone for the third time, anger began to consume Suki. She knew it was irrational for her to be upset, but she couldn't help it. She missed him and she wanted to find a way to make it work. Suki made a mental note to reach out to Simone so they could talk, and Simone would hopefully have some pointers on how it was Suki could get back into her brother's good graces.

"Suk, did you hear me?" Jinx called out.

"No. I'm sorry, babe. What did you say?" Suki asked, turning to see him staring at her.

"I said we're here," Jinx repeated.

Suki looked out the window and sure enough, they had pulled up in front of the restaurant where they were having their date night at. Suki was partially hoping Jinx canceled on her like he normally did so he could go do God's knows what or who. But the one time Suki wanted him to be a bad husband, he chose to keep his word to her. Suki scoffed at herself because two months ago she would have given anything for Jinx to be giving her the attention he was, but now, she was hoping he ignored her so she could chase behind another man. Yeah, she was losing it.

Get your shit together, Suk, Suki scolded herself.

Pushing all thoughts of Cheeko to the back of her mind, Suki allowed herself to focus on her husband and their date. Suki saw the line of people forming outside and was so happy Jinx had made them a reservation. It took them less than ten minutes to be seated and Suki was happy, because her shoes were not made to be walked in for long periods of time.

"You look nice tonight," Jinx complimented. "And you smell good too."

"Thank you, baby," Suki replied.

Guiding her to her chair, Jinx pulled it out for her, and Suki had to hide the shocked expression on her face. Suki couldn't remember the last time Jinx had done something nice like that for her. Maybe Jinx was trying to change his ways for the better. She still hadn't admitted she knew about his second life, and she knew if they were ever going to get to a better place, she'd have to confront him about it. But now in the situation she was in with Cheeko, Suki couldn't truly be as angry as she wanted to be because she had been keeping time with another man, and even though she hadn't fucked him, she would have if he didn't have sense enough to stop her.

When Suki allowed herself to focus on Jinx's company, she had to admit she was enjoying her time with him. Jinx kept her laughing and a part of her remembered what made her fall for him in the first place.

"Ain't this about a bitch," Jinx grumbled under his breath, looking at something behind where Suki was sitting.

"What's wrong, baby?" Suki questioned, prepared to turn around, but the smell that hit her nose stopped her in her tracks.

Dior Sauvage.

"Funny seeing you here."

It had only been two days, but his voice sounded like music to her ears. Suki's heart sped up in her chest and she could feel Cheeko's looming presence standing over her. Suki would have never pegged Cheeko as the type to blow up her spot, but now here she was, ready to face the music.

"Small world, right?" Jinx replied, plastering a fake smile on his face.

Confusion etched on Suki's face as she realized Cheeko wasn't speaking to her when he approached their table.

"Baby, I would like to introduce you to a colleague of mine," Jinx started, standing to his feet.

Without turning around, Suki placed her hand in Jinx's outstretched hand and had to stop her knees from shaking as she let him pull her to her feet. Suki prayed Cheeko wouldn't put her on blast, but the moment she turned around all color left Suki's face as she laid eyes on Cheeko standing next to a woman. Suki's eyes roamed the woman's face and body, and she was beautiful. Suki's eyes darted to Cheeko's face, but his was expressionless as he stared back at her.

"Suki, this is Cheeko. Cheeko, this is my wife, Suki," Jinx introduced. "My bad, Cheeko, I didn't know you had a girl. How you doing? You can call me Jinx."

Before Cheeko could open his mouth to respond, the woman began talking instead.

"Nice to meet you both. My name is Yesenia. I'm Cheeko's fiancée."

To Be Continued...

Made in United States
Orlando, FL
03 March 2023

30639434R00093